SHUGORO YAMAMOTO

The Flower Mat

translated by
Mihoko Inoue &
Eileen B. Hennessy

CHARLES E. TUTTLE COMPANY
Rutland, Vermont & Tokyo, Japan

Representatives

For Continental Europe:
BOXERBOOKS, INC., *Zurich*

For the British Isles:
PRENTICE-HALL INTERNATIONAL, INC., *London*

For Canada:
HURTIG PUBLISHERS, *Edmonton*

For Australasia:
BOOK WISE (AUSTRALIA), PTY. LTD.
104-108 Sussex Street, Sydney

PZ
3
. Y 142
. F1

*Published by the Charles E. Tuttle Company, Inc.
of Rutland, Vermont & Tokyo, Japan
with editorial offices at
Suido 1-chome, 2-6, Bunkyo-ku, Tokyo*

*Copyright in Japan, 1977
by Charles E. Tuttle Co., Inc.*

*Library of Congress Catalog Card No. 76-6031
International Standard Book No. 0-8048 1181-4*

First printing, 1977

Printed in Japan

Table of Contents

Introduction

IN RECENT years it has become increasingly fashionable to proclaim the end of national particularities and the gradual extension over the globe of standardized habits of thinking, feeling, and consuming. While this vision of the evolution of human society is an oversimplification, it is nevertheless true that if Kipling had been born only a decade or two later he might never have written the famous words, "East is East, and West is West, and never the twain shall meet."

Shugoro Yamamoto (1903–1967) was a man of our century. To read his novel, *The Flower Mat,* however, is to be plunged back into a time when East and West were indeed two completely different worlds. In the West it was the decade of the 1760s. In Japan, where the events related in the novel take place, it was approximately the 165th year of the Tokugawa period, very early in the seven-year reign of the Empress Go-Sakuramachi at the imperial capital of Kyoto.

More important, however, the tenth Tokugawa shogun, Ieharu, was now ruling throughout the land. The early shoguns had been generals and military deputies of the emperor. But since the Tokugawa family had come to power in 1603, the shogunate had gradually developed into a hereditary office that became the center of power in Japan, surpassing in authority the emperor himself. Under the rule of the Tokugawa shoguns the old social and political organization of Japan was molded into a unified and efficient state.

Not even the power of the Tokugawa shoguns, however, was able to prevent the gradual development of Japanese society, starting around the middle of the eighteenth century, along lines that were finally (in 1868) to lead to the end of the Tokugawa shogunate and the beginning of the Meiji era. The old feudal, "natural" economic system was gone, having been replaced by a money economy which would weaken the economic strength of the samurai, the ruling social class, and bring about the breakdown of the earlier, rigid class hierarchies.

The samurai had originally been warrior-farmers. Gradually, however, the samurai had ceased to be farmers and had tended to settle permanently in the castle towns, where they frequently found employment as administrators in the local government.

The Flower Mat relates the events of one year in the life of just such a samurai family, the Kugatas, when they become entangled in the intrigues surrounding the adoption of an heir to succeed the ruling *daimyo*. The latter is in this case one of the *daimyo,* or lords, of what was then known as Mino Province and is today Gifu Prefecture near Nagoya in central Honshu.

The tale of the reversals and ultimate vindication of the Kugata family is as timeless and universal as the human race itself. But the social structure and the background of feeling and philosophy which are so successfully portrayed in *The Flower Mat* are peculiar to Japan—perhaps even peculiar to the Japan of an earlier age.

Here we find ourselves in a family-oriented society in which the whole is greater than any of its individual components, a society whose members are motivated almost exclusively by a sense of duty—duty to family, to clan, to ruler, to a spiritual ideal higher than that of personal fulfillment. The needs of the individual are completely subordinate to those of the larger world of which he is a part.

Ichi, the instrument of the Kugata family's salvation, appears as the ideal Japanese woman of that time. She exists, and is valued, not for herself as an individual but as a loyal wife completely devoted to her husband and his family. Affection, whether between two people of opposite sex or between members of the family, is expressed not in terms of feeling or passion (no matter how highly spiritualized) but as a matter of supreme kindness, courtesy, and devotion to others' welfare.

The Western reader looks in vain, then, for traces of the conflicts and passions that dominate Western literature. At first their absence may puzzle and disconcert him. By the time he reaches the end of *The Flower Mat,* however, he experiences a strange feeling akin to solace and assuagement. There is something curiously soothing in this vision of a world motivated by quiet affection and devotion to simple, spiritual values rather than strong physical drives, material desires, and the urge for individual fulfillment.

—THE TRANSLATORS

The Flower Mat

IMPORTANT CHARACTERS

The Kugata Family:

ICHI, a daughter of the Okumuras who became a member of the Kugata family when she married the eldest son, Shinzo

SHINZO, Ichi's husband

ISO, Ichi's mother-in-law

TATSUYA, Shinzo's younger brother

KYUNOSUKE, Shinzo's youngest brother

NOBU, Ichi and Shinzo's daughter

The Okumura Family:

Ichi's mother

KASHO, Ichi's father

BENNOSUKE, Ichi's brother

LORD TODA, the *daimyo* (ruler) of Ogaki, a town in Mino Province (present-day Gifu Prefecture)

JOSUKE, a rich farmer in Ogasa village near the border of Lord Toda's territory

GEN, Josuke's wife

TEIJIRO, the owner of Minojin House in Shimada village near Ogasa

MANKICHI, the manager of the Minojin House workroom that produces flower mats

MOZAEMON, a farmer in Morishima, across the border from Ogasa

Prologue

IT IS SAID that the town of Ogaki in Mino Province was given its name, which means "great wall," following the erection of a massive stone rampart. This wall was later incorporated into the castle of the ruling *daimyo* to protect it from the floods that were quite numerous in the area due to the presence of the Kiso, Nagara, and Ibi rivers.

In the fourth year of the Horeki period, which is to say 1754, or about ten years before the events of our story, the Shimazu family, lords of Satsuma Province in Kyushu to the south, had been directed by the shogunate to carry out difficult flood-control work on the river embankments below Ogaki. Before the work was completed, however, the original budget of some thirty million *ryo* had multiplied nine times, and the hazardous work itself had left more than thirty of the

Note: This Prologue was originally the first chapter of Part II in the Japanese text. It has been adapted and placed here for the sake of the Western reader.

clan's samurai vassals, the *hanshi,* either dead or wounded. Yukie Hirata, a *karo,* or principal retainer, of the Shimazu clan, and forty-five of his samurai subordinates acknowledged their responsibility for the extraordinary cost overrun and loss of life; their suicides were an unprecedented tragedy.

Although flood disasters decreased considerably after this project's completion, the Ogaki area was not yet entirely safe, and when it rained more heavily and longer than usual, the town flooded near the upper reaches of the Satsuma construction area; even washouts of the great castle walls were not unusual. The town expended quite a large sum each year on river improvement, and the chief vassals from Ogaki took turns managing the work.

Over the years stories of these chief vassals' mismanagement and political corruption began to circulate. Inspection of the construction site was not duly carried out, and the construction budget constantly increased. The rise in property taxes to make up this sum finally brought many people to question the wisdom of allocating any more funds for this project.

The *daimyo,* Lord Toda, required by the Tokugawa shogunate to spend most of his time in the distant capital of Edo, appointed Toneri Otaka as *kuni-garo,* the chief vassal who would rule over the Ogaki area in his stead. Otaka was capable, talented, and possessed an extraordinary nature, as rising to such a position from the rank of *uma-mawari,* or samurai of the lord's horse guard, clearly demonstrated. Such a promotion would have been quite impossible for a man who was merely clever, smooth talking, or skilled at winning the confidence of others.

But the fairness of any system is easily destroyed when those who hold positions of authority begin to take themselves into consideration first or become motivated by power and profit. This was particularly true in Ogaki, where Toneri Otaka's ten-year grip on such an important position was in fact due to the support of the older families and other chief vassals of the clan. That certain advantages accrued to them is unquestioned, as is the fact that a cancer was spreading throughout the Ogaki government.

Lord Toda, at thirty-nine, ought to have been in the full flower of manhood, but he instead seemed in poor health and neglectful of clan government. His long term as *sosha-ban** was undoubtedly one of the reasons for this, as was the task, assigned him by the shogunate, of informing all the other *daimyo* that the new shogun, Ieharu, would recognize their holdings. The position of *sosha-ban* had been a tremendous strain on body and mind, and dealing with the various lords had been both a delicate and difficult matter. Lord Toda's reward for his efforts had been the gift of a sword from Ieharu and a steadily declining state of health.

---

* *Sosha-ban:* an official of the Tokugawa shogun charged with introducing the samurai to the shogun at festivals, with reading aloud the list of gifts given by the shogun, and with similar tasks. The office, created in 1632, was abolished in 1862.

Called Tokujiro as a child, Lord Toda had become the ruler of the clan at the age of seven and had taken in marriage Masaäki Hotta, who had borne him one son and five daughters. Only three daughters had survived to adulthood, however, and, owing to his poor health, Lord Toda was now beset by his vassals with suggestions regarding the adoption of a male heir to succeed him. To the great disgust of the people, these periods of succession had always generated struggles between new and old political factions, but in a few cases such struggles had actually led to reform of clan politics, since the adoption of an heir provided the perfect opportunity to begin the often necessary innovations in the government.

Seeing the struggle through to a successful conclusion was not always an easy matter, however, and in this conservative and feudalistic age, the more forceful approach often demanded an appropriate sacrifice. Yet if the reformists, who could always be counted on to make some sort of move, dealt with the problem systematically, there was a greater chance of good results for the government.

A clique consisting of Geki Ohara in Ogaki and Yazaemon Suzuki and Shingobe Hori, the two chief vassals in Edo, was proceeding in just this manner. They did not rush into things hastily but carefully built up a firm foundation, sparing neither time nor trouble in the hope that they would be able to rid the clan government of its recent corruption. They assigned Gorobe Toda (no relation to the lord) to spy on Kasho Okumura, a *karo,* and placed people in all the key positions. They thus took every measure necessary to secure their success.

Shinzo Kugata was in a position which made him important to this clique. It was his job, as a subordinate of the superintendents of the treasury, to handle general accounting matters—a most convenient position from which to guard against the mishandling of funds by those in power. This post had been held by the Kugata family for generations, and Toneri Otaka and his group must have felt a bit awkward in Shinzo's presence. But he was gentle and in fact looked stupidly honest. Moreover, since the parties in power did not dream of the existence of a clique preparing to fight them, they exercised little caution. Kasho Okumura had even married his beloved daughter, Ichi, to Shinzo.

Part One

1

SINCE the age of twelve or thirteen, Ichi had suffered from a recurrent eye infection with the coming of spring. She had forgotten about it lately, thanks to the change in her life created by her marriage to Shinzo Kugata. But shortly after the cherry trees at the castle had bloomed, her husband told her, "Your eyes are red." When she looked at herself in the mirror, she saw that the ailment had indeed begun again.

It could be said that she had weak eyes. If she devoted all her energy to sewing or read a book printed in small characters, her eyes would soon water or her eyelids begin to twitch. If she continued reading or sewing, it was not unusual for her vision to cloud, and she would be uncomfortable.

"You'd better not sew any longer," Iso, her mother-in-law, told her. "Your eyes are apt to be affected when you're expecting a baby, even if that's not the reason."

"I've had eye trouble since I was small. It will

somehow heal by itself if I can get through this season," Ichi answered.

Her reserved answer was a result of the constraint she still felt toward her mother-in-law, for she had been married only seven months. And yet, already Ichi had won a kind of self-confidence. Since she had become a member of the Kugata family she was enjoying every day; her life was full of a high-spirited, cheerful atmosphere, and she could feel that her body and mind were unfettered. She felt as if something that had not budded while she was still with her parents had suddenly begun to blossom.

This might have been because her family's discipline had been too strict and also because, being an only daughter and the last of five children, she had been pampered by her family. By nature she was not very strong; because of her family's overindulgence, she had never had any confidence in her health and had come to fret over even the most minor ailments.

But things were quite different in the Kugata household. Her husband, Shinzo, her mother-in-law, Iso, and her brothers-in-law, Tatsuya and Kyunosuke, were easygoing, simple people and were seldom fussy about things. They were also very liberal, unusual for a samurai family, and never assumed a haughty attitude. It was a foregone conclusion that you would be encumbered with constant cares for a time after you married, and not even Ichi could say that she had not experienced this. But it was only for a short time, and as soon as she had become familiar with the personality of this family, she felt a relieved, easy feeling. She stopped catching colds easily, and her arms and legs began to grow plump. Certainly she would be able to recover from her chronic eye infection.

"If you say so, all right. But please don't try too hard," her mother-in-law said, not forcing her to stop sewing.

That evening her brother-in-law Kyunosuke found out about her eyes and became excited.

"You're too easygoing, mother. In general, newly married wives who are expecting a baby no longer have to sew. You should do the same, sister," he said, turning to Ichi. "You'd better put away that fine work, and I seriously think you should go to a doctor soon."

"You're very knowledgeable about such matters," Iso said as she looked smilingly at her third son. "But what you're talking about has to do with the period after childbirth, doesn't it?"

"What? After childbirth?" He appeared embarrassed, and glanced quickly at his brothers.

Shinzo forced a smile and said, "Anyway, he always jumps to conclusions." Tatsuya, his face ever peaceful, nodded in agreement.

The personalities of these three brothers were clearly revealed in this trifling matter. Shinzo was uncommunicative, quiet in most respects, the kind of man who could take care of the smallest details in any situation. Tatsuya, the second brother, was round and plump of body and face, phlegmatic, and eternally smiling. He was fat and found it troublesome to move about, and his manner of talking was also slow. More-over, what he said was often funny, and his family often burst out laughing at his remarks. Some time previ-ously he had gone to see Sasamaki, his colleague in a group that practiced spear throwing. He was under the impression that his friend was only sick in bed, but actually Sasamaki had died. Upon returning home, Tatsuya told his family about his friend, saying, "They identified his sickness well enough, but when they treated him for it he became rather dead." This had made Shinzo and Iso laugh.

Kyunosuke was never silent on such occasions. Even then he had made fun of his brother's speech, saying that Tatsuya's talk was more amusing than the Zen dialogues.

"He died because they took good care of him. In short, he might have been saved if they hadn't taken care of him. To say that he became 'rather' dead is especially solemn," Kyunosuke had said.

Tatsuya had narrowed his eyes and smiled wordless-ly. The next day Kyunosuke had looked at Tatsuya as he was leaving the house and said, "Aren't they holding the rather funeral at Sasamaki's today?" Since then the word "rather" had become a frequently used word in the family.

This trick of tripping up people, together with a hasty temper and a stubborn nature, revealed Kyuno-suke's personality. He was quite talkative, but his movements were also quick, and he was said to be the most resourceful of the three brothers. Unlike

Tatsuya, who was twenty-four and just living at home, Kyunosuke, twenty-two, was working in the finance department, thanks to a patron in the person of one Chudayu Yoshihara, who was in charge of revenue. Kyunosuke had obtained his position two years ago, and even after Yoshihara had left for Edo as secretary to the lord of the House of Edo, Kyunosuke continued to be quite popular in the office.

It was to Kyunosuke that Ichi had first grown close after joining this family. He was four years older than she, but showed no sign of it. In any event he took good care of her, calling her "elder sister, elder sister."* Since he had importuned her for pocket money no more than ten days after her arrival, it was perhaps quite natural that she was beginning to feel at home with him. After that he asked her for pocket money about once every ten days, and she always smilingly handed it over, since she had received quite a large sum from her mother.

"What are you going to use it for?" she would ask. "If you need more, I can give it to you in a lump sum."

"Well, this is enough for now. Pocket money has a certain fascination when I get it bit by bit."

This was the type of conversation they carried on. Actually, Kyunosuke was earning money at the office. Tatsuya, who was idly living at home, might have done

---

* "Elder sister" (*onesan*) is what one would call the wife of an elder sibling, even if one is older than the woman.

well also. But Tatsuya was quite phlegmatic and did not have the wit or the inclination to find out what his younger brother was doing.

Ichi's eyes, which she had thought would heal easily, were not doing well at all. Since they began to water frequently after becoming red, she stopped doing fine work and resumed going to her eye doctor, Sekitai, for treatment. The treatment consisted merely of washing and checking her eyes, so after going to the doctor four or five times, she sent a servant for the medicine and administered the treatment herself, as she used to do while she was still living with her parents.

The dullness of her days, however, bothered her more than her eyes. When she was still single, she had paid little attention to her health and had read many books, often stealing away to her room. But now, as a bride, she could not shut herself up in her room all the time. Yet she was uncomfortable as she absent-mindedly watched her mother-in-law, who was doing sewing or similar work. In the morning she could finish her cleaning in about two hours. Since the family had servants, there was nothing for her to do before and after meals. Once in a while she would go to her mother-in-law's room and talk with her while making tea, but mostly she sat at the window of her room and spent the day looking out at the garden.

On one occasion, while she was having a difficult time enduring these boring hours, a messenger arrived from her family, the Okumuras, and informed her that they wished her to visit them, since her mother was ill in bed. Since Ichi had visited her only at New Year's and because she had plenty of free time, she decided to go, after asking Iso's permission. But while she was choosing a gift for her mother and wondering which kimono to wear, the hands of the clock crept around almost to noon.

"You'd better have lunch before you go, since you're already late," Iso told her. "If you go there now, I'm afraid you'll cause them trouble."

"I don't think so, but perhaps I will have lunch before I go."

Kyunosuke unexpectedly returned from the office while she was talking with Iso. As he passed along the corridor greeting them, he saw that his sister-in-law was wearing a formal kimono. He stopped and asked, "Oh, are you going out?"

Hearing that she was going to visit her mother, he bowed his head, as if there were something he could not quite understand. Then, as if thinking better of it and gazing into her eyes, he asked, "You are coming back today, aren't you?"

Naturally it was her intention to return that day, but since he sounded as if he wanted to make sure of this, Ichi felt that she was being accused; she answered that she would return by evening.

"What's the matter?" Iso asked, looking at her third son. "It seems very early. Aren't you feeling well?"

"Well, we're having a meeting of my colleagues

this afternoon. Since I'm in a hurry, won't you have the servants prepare lunch for me?"

With this Kyunosuke was about to leave, but he turned to Ichi once again and said, this time in a normal tone of voice, "Please give them my best regards. In particular, please tell Bennosuke that I'm longing to be able to see the *Seishukufu*."

"*Se-i-shu-ku-fu* . . . is that it?"

"Yes, that's right. It's a table of twenty-eight constellations which gives them names like the Eastern Seventh constellation with thirty-two stars or the Northern Seventh constellation with fifty-one stars. If you just tell him that, he'll understand."

Bennosuke was Ichi's brother, but she had never heard that he was studying such a thing. However, she merely thought that he was studying something new and strange. She left the house at the southeast gate.

The sunshine was dazzling, and the temperature was high. Even with her parasol, Ichi started perspiring after walking just a short distance. She noticed that the street was quite dusty because of the long drought. To get to the Okumura house she had to detour through the main gate of the castle and go almost halfway around it. It was not a long distance, but the light reflecting from the dry street hurt her eyes. After walking for a time, she would stop and wipe her eyes with a red silk cloth or close them and rest for a while. Thus the walk took longer than expected, and when she reached her parents' home she was so covered with perspiration that she had to change her undergarments.

2

 AS SOON as she reached the house she ordered Tami, a maid, to prepare hot water for her bath.

Tami was a farm girl of seventeen with a sunken face. She was not noted for her quick wit, but her extreme talkativeness appealed to Ichi. While Ichi listened, Tami would chatter aimlessly about nothing in particular, appearing perfectly happy as long as she could talk.

Ichi listened to her tales of customs and events in her native village, stories she had heard many times before. Some of these stories caused Ichi to blush, but Tami herself seemed to feel that they were quite natural, despite their occasional indecency.

"Oh, you've gained weight," Tami began as soon as Ichi went into the bathroom. "Your breasts look different now, don't they! When I washed you the last time, they weren't even as large as fists. And your back and hips . . . oh my, my!"

"You shouldn't talk so much about my body, Tami, you embarrass me. Put this hot water into the pail."

"You shouldn't be embarrassed about becoming so

beautiful. If you are, . . . now the younger lady,* I think she should . . ." And Tami launched into news about the wife of Ichi's eldest brother and about Ichi's brothers, adding that the retainer had had a child, that their dog Tachi had grown old, that a guest who was famous for his fondness for saké and drunkenness had fallen from the veranda and gotten a bump on his head, that she herself had received a marriage proposal, that she had no intention of marrying the man since she knew he was a good-for-nothing, that as many as three of the rose mallows in the garden had died this year. She continued with one thing and another, and by the time Ichi had washed and changed into her kimono she knew everything that had happened in the house since New Year's. Her ears were ringing. There was strict discipline in this house, and no one but Ichi would listen to Tami's chatter. She thought that Tami must have saved up these stories for her, and she could not scold the girl.

Ichi went to see her mother, who was sitting beside the bedding. Her mother's complexion had not changed, and she did not look like a sick person. Ichi's sister-in-law Kayo was preparing tea and cakes.

"Oh, my, your eyes have started again," her mother said, paying no attention to Ichi's inquiries. "I'm afraid this eye disease is going to be a lifelong habit

---

* "The lady" is the wife of the master of the house, e.g., Ichi's mother. "The younger lady" here is the wife of a son of the family, i.e., one of Ichi's sisters-in-law. A married son and his family always lived in his parents' home.

with you. Are you visiting your doctor, Sekitai? Hmm . . . I guess the Kugata family lives differently, but you're not taking care of yourself, are you? You look worse than you usually do."

Though Ichi insisted that she had not done any fine work for a long time and that she was even troubled because she had nothing to do, her mother's suspicious expression remained.

Ichi's father and oldest brother were at work, but two of her brothers, Heizaburo and Bennosuke, soon appeared. They looked as meticulous as ever, sitting so straight that even the pleats of their *hakama** did not crumple. Their conversation covered conventional subjects, and they ran out of topics after only one cup of tea.

The brothers soon left. But Ichi had detected a subtle change in the atmosphere of this house. Her mother and brothers had not asked her about the Kugata family and very plainly indicated that they wished to avoid the subject when Ichi was about to tell them about her in-laws. Her mother's remark that Ichi must not have been able to take care of herself had a critical tone somehow.

"Please stay with us for a while," her mother said casually. "While I'm not seriously ill, somehow I feel weak. I've been having sleepless nights, and I feel depressed."

"But I can't stay, mother. I don't have permission

* *Hakama:* a pleated skirt for men's formal wear.

from my husband, and moreover I came here with the intention of going back by evening."

"You can send a message by the maid you brought with you, and I'll also send them a message. Moreover, with those infected eyes, you've got to have a good rest."

"Yes, mother," Ichi answered vaguely, and stood up. "I heard the rose mallows died. Were they infested with vermin?"

"Father replanted them because he wanted to enlarge the chrysanthemum garden. It might have been all right if it had rained. . . . I guess this long drought has damaged them. But only three of them have died."

Ichi went down to the garden.

It was said that the Okumura family belonged to the rich families among the *roshoku* or chief vassals. Since the Okumuras were samurai, their everyday life was humble, and their wealth could not have been detected from their way of life. But their stone garden, believed to have been copied from the garden of the Ryoan temple in Kyoto, and the construction of the house, which gave the impression of being palatial, seemed to be indicative of wealth. Ichi's father claimed he had selected such construction because this land suffered from flooding about once every five years (this figure was something of an exaggeration). But the same good taste was visible in their paintings and vases for incense, tea, and flowers, and in their furniture. Every object was carefully chosen, dignified, and expensive, and there was not a single one which did not have an interesting history.

Ichi had been about five years old when her parents said, "This house is a bit too harsh for a girl." They had made her a flower garden at the side of the house. Since then she had not visited the back garden and had no interest in seeing it.

The house has an atmosphere of quiet dignity everywhere and in every object, Ichi thought as she walked toward the flower garden. How different from the Kugatas—both the house and the people.

In the Kugata house there were many stains on the walls from old floods, and gashes in the pillars. The dishes, while beautiful, were not expensive. A black-and-white brush painting of a pine tree hung permanently in an alcove, and there was nothing which could be classified as an antique. Everything in the house, however, was always neat and clean. Not a few of the things which Ichi had brought with her in her trousseau—an oil vase from the Philippines, coral, jade, or tortoise-shell hair pieces, a dressing box made of sandalwood, and other small items and dresses—clashed with the Kugata family's decor or scheme of things. Ichi had wisely put most of these things away in a storage chest. Now the difference between these two families was impressed upon her more clearly.

But what was the real reason for the big change in her family's attitude toward the Kugatas? What was behind her mother's suggestion that Ichi remain with her for a while? Kyunosuke had asked whether she was returning that day; his attitude too had seemed different. Something must have happened. These were not simple coincidences.

When Ichi reached the flower garden, she saw Bennosuke coming toward her, and she was seized by an uneasy feeling.

Bennosuke had the most delicate build of all the brothers, and his complexion was not good. He had deeply knit eyebrows and a gloomy expression. Normally he was gentle, but if he got angry he had a hot temper which nobody could control. Being the nearest to her age, this was the brother to whom she was closest.

Bennosuke came close to her, avoiding her eyes, and asked in a low voice, "Did mother tell you anything?"

"She asked me to stay with her for a while," Ichi said. "She was very insistent, as if she had some strong reason for it. Has something happened between our family and the Kugatas? Do you know something, Bennosuke?"

"Return to the Kugatas immediately." He was avoiding her eyes. "You'd better not come here for a while."

"You say I'd better not come here . . . then something has happened."

"I guess it will blow over peacefully. It's nothing you should worry about. Go home without saying anything to mother." He looked at his sister. "I think you've gained weight. I hope there's nothing wrong with your health."

"I have a message from Kyunosuke. He says that he's longing to see the *Seishukufu*."

Bennosuke's eyes widened and looked astonished or frightened. "You'd better leave right away," he said. He left in the direction from which he had come.

Ichi was unable to understand the situation. But her uneasiness was growing, and she decided to follow her brother's advice without delay. His suggestion that she leave without saying anything to their mother hastened her decision.

She quietly called her maid, who had been waiting for her in the servants' room, and told her to get ready. She went out by the side gate, still wearing the kimono into which she had changed. She did not like to leave her wet things there, but she was sure that if she went in to get them she would be noticed by her sister-in-law, so she gave up the idea.

She left the house without being seen, but she was frightened, and hurried along the street as if she were being chased by someone. Her heart beat rapidly, and her eyes began to water, since the sun was still bright. Ichi wiped away the tears with the red cloth, but she was unable to wipe away her dark foreboding.

What has happened? What will happen now? she wondered. Should I have said good-bye to my mother? Why did Bennosuke look so surprised when he heard the word *Seishukufu*? I don't understand. But something unusual and possibly dreadful is going on.

"You're not walking fast enough." Ichi hurried her maid along with frequent urgings.

3

 ICHI'S uneasy feeling persisted for days, and she could not talk about it to anyone. She constantly studied the demeanors of her husband and Kyunosuke, searching for a hint or a sign of what was going on, but to no avail.

Her nerves were strained; she would leap to her feet at the slightest sound, and had terrible dreams in the night, when she would be mercifully awakened by her husband. But since nothing happened and the Kugata family seemed little changed, her worries gradually eased.

She thought about her own family, which she had left without a word. She had immediately sent them a message that she had become ill. Her mother had sent her the bundle of clothes left behind, with a note urging Ichi to take care of herself. The messenger had returned the following day and inquired about her health.

When she told Kyunosuke that she had given his message to her brother, he too seemed unconcerned, saying, "Oh, thanks." When she put these things together in her mind, it all seemed very natural, and the only definite cause for her anxiety appeared to be Bennosuke's words. Now she was not even certain that the atmosphere of the Okumura house had changed.

Since the season of young leaves, Ichi had acquired the habit of waking up at midnight and being unable to go back to sleep for some time. She would lie wide awake and, should she try to force herself to sleep, would perspire in a strange way. Then she would feel a strong urge to see her husband's face, and her heart would become heavy.

Her husband slept in the next room, which was separated from hers by a sliding door. She would feel relieved if she could hear him sleeping or breathing, but he always slept peacefully, in a way that would have impressed even Iso, and he slept so quietly that it sometimes made her wonder whether he was awake. She suppressed her desire to see him, thinking that it was simply too indecent, but one night she couldn't suppress it any longer.

She got up and opened the door quietly. A light from the floor lamp, which had been dimmed, was shining softly on Shinzo, sleeping on his back with the bed cover pulled up to his chin. His long, tight face with clearly marked eyebrows made people feel his strong, almost cold will, but when he was sleeping his lips became tender, and a soft warmth appeared on his long-lashed eyes and on his cheeks, a warmth which tempted her to go close to him.

Ichi felt a strong thirst in her throat, a kind of burning, irritated feeling, and an aching itch in her body. But suddenly and without any apparent reason, a terrible suspicion seized her, a feeling that her husband was not interested in her and that he would someday go away. She shook her head, saying to herself that this was impossible, but thoughts shook her mind like the shout of someone she could not see.

What kind of a person are you for this man? Does being a husband, or being a wife, really link the destiny of two people so tightly? What does it really mean, being husband and wife? What am I worth to my husband? Have I really been loved by my husband?

Ichi began to tremble. A man named Shinzo Kugata existed far, far from her; they were united only by a frail bond which could easily snap. Her husband had never loved her, and would never love her, and he must go away somewhere, leaving her behind. . . .

Her growing sadness caused Ichi to sob. Sitting on the floor and pressing both hands to her eyes, she cried with abandon. Shinzo heard her and turned to her. He did not speak at once, but watched in puzzlement. Then he asked in a gentle voice, "What are you doing here at this time of night?"

"Oh!" Ichi almost leaped to her feet.

Shinzo halfway rose from the bed and asked, "Ichi! What's happened? Are you ill?"

"No, no." She shook her head and tried to stand, moving backward. The thing which had filled her mind was now flowing out like a torrent. She fell forward on her face, wracked with sobs, caring nothing about her embarrassing position. "It's nothing," she cried.

Shinzo watched intently. The fresh curves of his wife's young body gave her a coquettish beauty in the dim light, a beauty filled with the life, power, and pride of a woman who had finished the ceremonial tying of the maternity obi at the beginning of the fifth month of pregnancy.

"You'll get cold if you stay there," said Shinzo, as if admonishing a child. "Come in here, I'll warm you." He turned back the corner of the bed cover.

"I shouldn't get in," she thought, "it's really too indecent." But despite her thoughts, Ichi's body was already sliding in next to her husband's.

How thankful she was later that she had had the power in her body to do this at the time! She had been able to experience a feeling which hitherto had not been fully awakened in her. It overwhelmed her with a powerful ecstasy, with convulsions not unlike those which accompany death, and it penetrated to the very depths of her body and mind. This sensation was so overwhelming that her whole mental outlook changed. A great surge of self-confidence, pleasure, and pride swept over her—pride in being Shinzo's wife.

Her habit of waking up at midnight, however, lasted for some time. Usually she waited a time for sleep to return, but whenever it seemed hopeless, she went to Shinzo for help. Her husband would smile at her as though dandling her like a baby, and would quietly make a place for her in his bed. Ichi would modestly slide in and lie close to him. Her husband's body heat and his rather strong body odor would encompass her so tightly that it was rather oppressive. She would be entranced with a feeling of great relief and incomparable happiness, and would close her eyes and sigh. Overcome by such sweetness and ecstasy, Ichi sometimes cried, pushing her head against her husband's chest.

"It's nothing," she said, seeking the hand of her wondering husband and still hiding her face. "There's nothing sad. I'm so happy. I'm so happy that it almost makes me sad, and tears come. Do you think there's something wrong with me?"

"Your health isn't normal," her husband said, stroking her back soothingly. "Did you feel something like that when you came here and cried the other night?"

"That was different. I don't know why, but that night I could think only sad things, and I couldn't do anything except cry."

"What sad things?"

"That you don't love me, that you will leave me someday. . . . When I think of it now, I wonder how I could even think such things." Ichi trembled. "I don't even want to remember it. I'm sure something was wrong with me."

Shinzo said nothing. He seemed on the verge of speaking, but suddenly knit his brows, and his lips twitched. He looked vaguely off into space and continued stroking his wife's back. Whenever he did this, Ichi's nerves would gradually calm down and she sometimes fell asleep.

"Well, go back to your bed and sleep," her husband told her softly. "I'm sure you can. Sleep well."

When the rainy season began, her eye condition almost cleared up. Since this had been a year of little rain, it had seemed there would be no rainy season at all, and the drought (which the old men said was the worst in more than ten years) continued. However, there were generous springs everywhere in the region, and there was little possibility of a crop failure in the event of a long drought. On the contrary, since there was danger of flooding if it rained too much, people were usually pleased by a dry rainy season.

About this time her husband and Kyunosuke seemed to become very busy. They would often go out after dinner and would come back from the castle at odd hours and sometimes not until the following day, explaining that they had been "on night duty." More unfamiliar guests began coming to the house.

Despite these occurrences, Tatsuya was as composed as ever. Because of his obesity he had a difficult time in the heat. He was never seen doing anything but noisily using his fan and, with a folded towel in his hand, constantly wiping off perspiration. Yet he would never try to forget about the heat by engaging in some activity or by looking for a shady place or a breeze. Even when the sun reached the place where he sat, he would never move to another place. He would gaze at the moving sun and continue gazing at it until it reached a part of his body, his legs, a shoulder, or his navel. Then he would sigh, move back a bit, and twirl the fan noisily, wiping off sweat with his other hand.

When Kyunosuke peeped into his room one day, Tatsuya was sitting with his back against the wall. The perspiration was rolling in beads down his red face. The sun was shining on him from his chest down, and he looked like a broiled lobster.

When Kyunosuke asked, "What are you doing in such a sunny place?" Tatsuya replied that he had been able to escape the sun so far, but "back of me is a wall. . . ."

"You shouldn't sit still like that, you should do something," Kyunosuke said, staring at his brother. "You'd better move around a bit. If you do something, you'll be able to forget about the heat."

"I think so too." Tatsuya displayed the fan and the towel he was holding to his younger brother. "But I have to fan with one hand and wipe sweat off with the other—so both my hands are occupied. I simply can't do anything else."

4

FOR A LONG time now there had been silence between the Okumura and Kugata households. Until the spring, some kind of visit or inquiry had passed between the two families about once every ten days, but since Ichi's visit home that day, communication had broken off. However, Ichi's mother still sent a messenger once in a while to inquire after her health and sent letters saying that she wanted Ichi to come to see her if she had time. However, Ichi's mind was still disturbed by Bennosuke's words, and she did not feel like visiting her mother. It seemed impossible that she should have become estranged from her parents like that. If she waited for a time and found that nothing had actually happened, she would easily be able to communicate with them again.

Around the middle of June, while she was thinking along these lines, a letter came from her father, addressed to Shinzo.

> Ichi's time is approaching, and I am happy to know that she is doing well. But since she is our only daughter, and since in addition it is her first child, we would like her to give birth at our house, if it is possible. There are many such cases, but in this case, since my wife and I (and particularly my wife) greatly desire it, I should appreciate your granting our request, selfish though it may be. Depending on your answer, we are ready to send someone to fetch her when it is convenient for you.

"My mother has no objections, but what do you think?" Shinzo asked, after he had let Ichi read the letter. "We should forget now about your hesitation and reserve. I want to know what you really want."

It was teatime, after supper, and Kyunosuke, Tatsuya, and Iso were also there. Ichi indicated that she wanted to think about it for a while, but soon answered firmly that she wanted to give birth in her husband's house and that she was not going back to her parents'. The truth was that she would have felt safer and more relaxed at her parents' house. As a girl she had often heard people say that "so-and-so is now at her parents' house to give birth," and there must have been a good reason for it. But again Ichi remembered Bennosuke's words and could not bring herself to say that she would go home.

"But don't you think your parents would feel bad, since they want you to go home?" Iso asked, as if she had not expected this answer from Ichi. "In any event, it's your first childbirth. I think you'll feel more secure when the time comes if you're with your parents."

"I don't think so," Kyunosuke said as if angry. "Since mother has had experience giving birth to and raising three children, and since we have enough servants, I don't think we should bother the Okumuras. I think that what Ichi said is right."

"That may be true, but you really feel helpless with the first childbirth, though Kyunosuke may not be able to understand this since he's a man."

"Anyway, think it over for a while and let me have your answer later," Shinzo told Ichi. "It's not something you should decide in a hurry, and it won't be too late after you've thought it over well. . . . No, Kyunosuke, that's all right," Shinzo added. "I know exactly what your opinion is."

Kyunosuke had been about to say something and seemed unhappy at being cut off. Only Tatsuya had been silent from the beginning, absorbed as usual in using his fan and wiping perspiration. When they had finished talking, however, he said something strange.

"I've heard they wrap hemp around a dog's belly, and then it can give birth to its young rather easily."

"Around a dog's belly?" Iso asked him, shocked. "Sometimes you say things we can't understand, Tatsuya. . . ."

"Since I heard it from someone, I don't know whether it's true or not. It's probably a superstition, but I heard that everyone does it."

"From whom did you hear this?" Iso asked.

"You know the old man named Josuke—the one who brings vegetables to the kitchen? . . . From that old farmer." Tatsuya blinked his puffy, drooping eyes. "And I also heard that Josuke's wife is very good at delivering babies. They say there will never be a mistake if his wife is asked to attend any dangerous childbirth."

Iso's eyes widened. "Why did you get into such a conversation? Isn't that old man a queer person to have told you such a thing!"

"Oh no, that old man and Tatsuya talk about anything," Kyunosuke said, coming to his brother's rescue. "When I was listening to him the other day, he was so proud of having made an eggplant bear 416 fruits. He was saying something about fertilizer, wasn't he, Tatsuya? Hasn't he been coming here for a long time?"

"Well, another old man named Heishichi had been coming here until year before last. Since Josuke is the successor to that man, it's been almost two years."

"Anyway, he's able to get along with Tatsuya. He chats for long hours, unaware that the greens he's brought are withering. You know, the other day . . ."

Ichi, thinking over Tatsuya's words, was moved. When she had heard about wrapping hemp around a dog's belly, she had almost laughed. But in his own way Tatsuya was showing concern about her.

Ichi also knew that the farmer would chat for long hours with Tatsuya whenever he came. He was a short, small old man with a flabby body, looking more like a retired townsman than a farmer. His clothes were neat, and the strings of his sedge hat were always white as though freshly washed. The farmer would sit on the stump of a paulownia beside the hut in which the firewood was stored, take out a tobacco case, old and worn and made of India leather, and talk and smoke simultaneously. His topics of conversation were never the same. He could be said to have a simple, honest personality. He always put the year, month, and date at the beginning of his conversation: "Since it was the Year of the Tiger, it must have been such-and-such year, such-and-such month, such-and-such day." That was his way of talking, and Tatsuya would listen with enjoyment from his room, leaning over the window or sitting on the window sill.

The Kugata family had always made it a practice to talk to everyone as equals, and when Ichi listened to the conversations between Tatsuya and Josuke, they sounded like conversations between friends. Now she could imagine them talking about a charm for easy delivery.

A few days later Ichi again told the family that she was not going back to her parents' house, and the Okumuras were informed through Shinzo. The wife of Chusai Yonezawa, a family doctor of the clan, was skilled at examining pregnant women, and Ichi had therefore been consulting her from the beginning of her pregnancy. Each time she was examined, the foetus had grown so well that the doctor's wife was satisfied, and Ichi was told that she was doing very well. She had been performing exorcisms on tabu days and trying to observe the prohibitions and warnings about foods, ways of sleeping, and compass directions. After she had definitely decided not to go back to her parents' house, she became more cautious and tried to avoid everything that pregnant women were said to detest, even though such sayings were probably only superstitions.

After the letter of refusal had been sent to the Okumuras, Ichi's mother sent her a letter together with an amulet to ensure an easy delivery.

I don't think it will happen, but if the baby refuses to come out at the time of delivery, you should write down the word "ISE" with India ink on white paper, and swallow the paper. The word "ISE" consists of the characters which mean "this is one who has power to be born," and it has long been said that to swallow it draws the grace of the gods remarkably well.

The letter also contained a *kaiba* (a dried sea fish resembling a dragon) and a cowrie shell, the name of which, *koyasugai,* means "safe delivery."

Since her husband was again late in returning from the castle, Ichi brought the objects to the living room after supper and showed them to him.

"Giving birth to a child is really something." Shinzo forced a smile. "This one is called *kaiba,* isn't it? What is this shell called?"

"They say it's a cowrie—*koyasugai.*"

"Hmm . . . *koyasugai.* The very name makes it a talisman. How are you going to use these two objects?"

"I will hold them in my hands . . ." But at that instant she was interrupted by the sound of someone walking in the garden, and she turned towards the window. Shinzo also turned.

"I am Gorobe Toda." A voice came through the straw screen hanging down over the veranda. He had evidently come in the back door and, seeing the light, had headed for the living room.

Shinzo stood up, exclaiming, and went out to the veranda.

"You're Toda from the Edo mansion, aren't you?"

"Yes, I am. I know it's impolite to call on you through the back door, but I have to hide from prying eyes. You don't mind?"

"No, not at all. Please come in."

"My feet are dirty. Where is the well?"

"No, we'll get water for you. Please come in just as you are."

Ichi, who had been listening to the whispered conversation, stood up to fetch water to wash the guest's feet. Her dark, uneasy feeling returned with this new development.

I should not ask the servant to do this, she thought.

She carried in the water and the basin for the guest to wash his feet. He was sitting in a corner of the veranda and was removing his straw sandals. The two men had been talking, and they suddenly fell silent when Ichi walked in. She left immediately. But Shinzo followed, and whispered, "I'll tell everybody about this later on, but don't tell them anything now. Just bring a change of clothes, and tea."

She brought in the things requested and glanced at the guest, who was a slender man of medium height, about thirty-three years old. She noticed that one of his front teeth was broken and that wrapped around his left arm was a cotton rag through which blood had oozed, probably from a wound.

"Shall I bring some medicine?" Ichi asked her husband.

Shinzo gestured no. "Tell Kyunosuke to come in here when he returns," he whispered. "You don't have to come until I call you."

Ichi, nervous now, returned to Iso's side and opened up the baby's cloth which she had begun to sew. But her nervousness increased, and soon she was unable to remain seated any longer.

"May I make tea?"

"All right." Iso, seated at her desk, was reading. She looked at Ichi through her glasses and yawned slightly. "Are there any cakes left?"

"I think we have only black candies."

"What is Shinzo doing now?"

"It looks as if he's checking into something."

5

WHILE she was preparing tea, Tatsuya came in, as was usual. Whenever she started to prepare tea Tatsuya would show up without fail, even when he had been in the garden. Ichi remembered a story which her nurse had told her when she was small about an old man who had a nose for good smells. Tatsuya reminded her of the story, and she smiled. The other members of the family saw nothing peculiar in his behavior. That they protected and treated each other kindly was another revelation of the family character. No one in the Kugata family was ever laughed at or scolded or accused. Almost everything would be passed over with the words "He's all right as he is." Protection and sympathy toward each other were at the root of their attitude.

"Strange—there are no mosquitoes in your room, mother." Tatsuya reached over to the candy bowl and picked out a black candy. "I think there aren't too many of them in Shinzo's or Kyunosuke's room. But as for my room, there's no difference between day and night; they just come and never leave. I wonder what they're thinking."

"That's because you're there all day, Tatsuya. They go in there because your odor has become attached to your room. It would be better if you burned mosquito incense, but you never do."

"You might be right. But don't you think even mosquitoes have likes and dislikes in eating? For example, this person doesn't taste good, or this man isn't so bad. . . ."

Kyunosuke returned home. When Ichi heard him at the front of the house, she quickly went and told him what her husband had said. Kyunosuke nodded, went into his mother's room with an innocent look on his face, and suddenly reached for the candies.

"I'm sorry I'm late."

"You often come home late nowadays," said Iso.

"That's because we're going to start checking the crops in the field soon," Kyunosuke answered. "Since the property tax is apparently going to be increased again this year, it's hard work to prepare the assessments."

"Increasing the property tax again—well, well," said Tatsuya. "If the property tax is increasing like that, I bet the farmers won't be able to live a very easy life."

Kyunosuke was about to say something, but he changed his mind. He got up and went into the back room.

After a time Shinzo came in. He picked up his tea-cup, but soon put it down and looked at Iso a bit uncertainly.

"I have a favor to ask of you," he said to his mother. "I want you to take in a boarder. What do you say to that?"

"What do you mean by a boarder?" Iso raised her eyes with a puzzled expression. "What kind of person is he?"

"He's lived a little too fast a life. Being the third son and having a strong personality, he ran away from home. But things would be all right if he apologized to his parents. He came in here through the back door and is now in my room."

"Well, I'm sorry to hear that. We don't mind having him at all, but this is a small house."

"Well, I'll let him use my room." Shinzo stood up. "And since he doesn't want his family to know where he is until he apologizes to them, please manage it somehow with the servants."

"Shouldn't I greet him?" Iso asked.

"Tomorrow will be all right. Ichi, won't you come with me?"

Ichi followed Shinzo. Instead of consulting her as he usually did, he gave her orders concerning the meals and bedding for the guest and told her to tell the servants that a relative was in the house. He also told her that the guest might stay with them about twenty days, depending on the circumstances.

That night after Ichi had gone to bed, the whispered conversation went on in her husband's room. It was an unusually close, humid night, and she was perspiring in the bed. The buzzing of mosquitoes around the netting disturbed her, as did low voices from the room beyond her own. She wiped away perspiration constantly, unable to sleep. And the night passed.

Around noon the next day a strong north wind began to blow, and soon the weather became stormy. After the long drought the trees and grass had become white as if covered with dust, but their glossy green color reappeared before Ichi's eyes, and they swayed with a sudden gust of wind as if they were dancing for joy.

Ichi was fond of rain and liked to watch it through the window. She felt herself revived. The clouds, the color of India ink with gradations into gray, were running fast from south to north in a low sky. Depending on the density of the clouds, the rain became scant or strong; it slapped trees, slapped houses, and slapped the ground, and everywhere made a thick gray splash.

Ichi had felt that her body was drying up, and that even her blood had become thicker. But while she watched the rain, her skin was thirstily absorbing moisture. Just as fresh moss holds water, she felt that her whole body was becoming richly damp with moisture.

While Ichi watched the rain with a feeling akin to intoxication, she remembered the man named Gorobe Toda. He used to visit the Okumura household six or seven years ago, bringing official business to her father, who at that time held the post of *karo,* or principal retainer. At one period he had shown up at the house almost every day. He must have known that Ichi was greatly loved by her family and especially by her father, Kasho, for he had brought flowers to her on several occasions. Of course she did not receive them herself, and her parents would not have allowed her to place flowers presented by her father's subordinate in her room, but the sweet white oleanders, mountain lilies, and wonderful yellow chrysanthemums were beautiful and left a lasting impression.

After a time the man had stopped coming, but she had a faint recollection of a story that he had been demoted to a post at Edo because he had done something wrong. It must be this same man who was in the Kugata home.

Even if this were the same man, there was nothing strange about it, she thought. But when she noted his condition now—wounded, hiding from prying eyes— there seemed an unfortunate distance, too, between the Ichi of the present and the Ichi who had received flowers from him years before. Her heart grew heavy.

"Well, well, you're sitting beside the window." Iso's loud voice cut into Ichi's silent thoughts. "Rain splatters are blowing in, aren't they! It's bad for your health. What are you doing here?"

"It's raining so magnificently, I was fascinated." Ichi was a little embarrassed. She blushed. "Oh, I've made the *tatami** so wet! What shall I do!"

"It's you who's important, not the *tatami*. You'd better change your clothes quickly. That's all right—I'll order the maid to clean it up." Then, calling after Ichi who was hurrying from the room, "Unless you dry your body thoroughly you'll catch cold."

The rain and the wind stopped around midnight. It had rained so hard during the early evening that they had feared flooding. But with the passing of the storm, the weather had turned unbelievably fine, and the moon dipping toward the west shone beautifully, as if **newly** polished.

Three guests had arrived during the storm and had talked for a long time with Ichi's husband and Kyunosuke in the room where Toda was staying. What they were talking about she of course did not know. Two had left around ten o'clock, and the third when the sky was growing lighter. Her husband had said good-bye to the third guest at the back door, but had not immediately reentered the house. This caused Ichi concern, and she got out from under the mosquito netting.

* *Tatami:* a thick straw matting about 3 ft. by 6 ft. used as a floor covering. It is still often used as a unit of measure for rooms, e.g., a 10-mat room.

The terrible thought came to her that her husband might have gone somewhere and she would never see him again, or that some extraordinary thing had happened and that his life was in danger. She was so wrought up that she forgot about being clad only in her nightgown, and she hurried outside in her bare feet. Her agitation was so great that her feet seemed barely to touch the ground. She hurried to the back door and found her husband standing by the garden fence in front of the door. Shinzo was alone. One hand was resting on the fence, and he was gazing at the moon. Ichi would not soon forget the outline of her husband's head and back as he stood gazing upward.

Shinzo turned slowly, and when he saw Ichi he went close to her.

"What a reckless thing to do! Why are you out here dressed like that?"

Ichi groaned and looked up at her husband. Her anguish changed quickly to relief and joy and to an overpowering love for her husband.

She threw herself into Shinzo's arms, sobbing. "Since you didn't come back at once, I was afraid that you might have gone somewhere or that something might have happened to you, and I couldn't remain in the room."

"You silly!" Shinzo put his arm around his wife and hugged her. "What are you frightened about? I'm only looking at the moon—it was so beautiful when I came out here to see my guest off. It's as clear as if it had been washed by rain."

"Please tell me, is some misfortune about to happen?" Ichi whispered, her head still pressed against his breast. "I've been so worried lately, constantly fighting an uneasy feeling. I know it's not my place to ask such a thing, but won't you please tell me what is going on?"

His arms held her more tightly, and his face, illuminated by the moon, assumed an expression almost of agony. He closed his eyes and pushed his face close to Ichi's, and was silent for what seemed like ages.

"A samurai cannot live only for himself and his family," he finally said. "This applies not only to samurai but to all human beings. Every man has an obligation to mankind in addition to himself and to his family. I am now trying to carry out one of these obligations, which concerns the government of this clan. Moreover, it has much to do with the happiness or unhappiness of our people."

"Just as I expected!" Ichi cried, drawing away from him. Her look turned from one of love to despair. "This has been going on after all. . . . Our life will soon be destroyed, won't it?"

"You must try to be calm. We're doing our utmost to avoid any tragedy. Since the problem isn't a difficult one, and since we've been working on it very carefully, I think it will be solved safely behind the scenes. We made a promise that we wouldn't rush things until we were assured of success."

"You've got to stop this, please!" Ichi shook her head. "There are many people here; I don't think this is your problem alone. And I can't live without you. Please think of the one who is going to be born and of your mother. Don't do anything to destroy the happiness of this family."

Shinzo looked at his wife as if she were a stranger. Her shy, oval face, generally regarded as beautiful, had changed completely. This woman with glittering eyes and twisted lips was not Ichi. This selfish, greedy face full of an animal instinct to hold onto what she had was not that of the woman he loved.

"Aren't you ashamed of yourself for saying such a thing, Ichi? Husband and wife, children, parents, brothers, home, a happy life—everyone wants these things, and it's hard to watch them being lost or destroyed. But we have to defend society from overthrow and destruction. Every human being has this duty, particularly the samurai, who are in a position to engage in politics. . . . Isn't it funny that you don't understand such an obvious thing, Ichi, even though you were brought up in a samurai family."

Shinzo gently held his wife close. "Well, lift your face and look up at the moon," he said. "Your nerves are on edge because your health isn't normal. Everything will soon be resolved safely. We're working on it, so you shouldn't be so worried. Just give birth to a healthy, good child. . . . Cheer up and look at the moon. This must be the first time you've ever looked at the moon this late in the evening."

Shinzo put his hand under his wife's chin, raised her head, and smiled at her.

How powerful, how dear, how beloved is my husband's moonlit face! Even if something happens, my husband belongs to me, Ichi thought. I shall never let him go—never.

She impulsively put her arms around her husband's neck and stretched to press her lips against his. Shinzo tried to avoid her passionate kiss but thought better of it and, embracing Ichi's trembling body, accepted the kiss, which tasted of tears.

* * *

Part Two

6

THE STRONG driving rain was followed by a heat wave which immediately dried up the earth, trees, and grass, as if the rain had never fallen. The streets had to be watered regularly to keep down the clouds of dust which rose thickly into the air.

The region had almost limitless underground springs, and pure water came to the surface in the city and the fields wherever wells had been dug. Ogaki's people would never be short of water, even if there was a long drought.

Of course the Kugata house had its own well, which despite its shallowness gave a generous supply of water that overflowed from the trough and imparted an illusion of coolness. Iso found it too cold, but it was Ichi's only relief from the heat, and she sometimes felt she could not endure a moment without it.

Note: In the original Japanese text, the section describing the political situation in Ogaki was the first chapter of Part II. Adapted for the Western reader, it appears at the very beginning of this translation.

Ever since her talk with her husband about the samurai's obligations, Ichi had been under a nervous strain which might have resulted from her physical condition. She was subject to sudden attacks of violent heartbeat and feelings of suffocation. Worse yet was her inability to fall asleep easily. Her sense of hearing became more acute, and she could hear voices or the movements of people two rooms beyond hers.

Yet nothing unusual was happening. The guest, Gorobe Toda, confined himself all day to his room, where he seemed to do everything in a languid reclining position. The regular visitors had by now decreased to three, and their visits had become less frequent—first every three days, then every five days. However, since Ichi did not know what was going on, she could not tell whether this change portended a good or bad turn of events, and her ignorance increased her uneasiness.

Around eleven o'clock one night, five or six days after the worst summer heat, she heard the unusual sound of high-pitched voices in the family room. The voices were so clear that from where she lay under the mosquito netting Ichi could distinguish the words.

She involuntarily sat up upon hearing the word *Seishukufu*. When she had gone to visit her mother in the spring, this unfamiliar word had been Kyunosuke's message to her brother, and she remembered it readily now because her present feeling was exactly like the uneasiness aroused in her at that time by Bennosuke's reaction to the message.

Ichi listened to the loud conversation with bated breath.

"This *Seishukufu* is worthless. Not only is it worthless—it's absurd."

"Why?" Kyunosuke asked. "The person who did it is a friend of mine. I know his work and I know him personally, and I know he's reliable."

"Maybe he's reliable, but this *Seishukufu* is absolutely useless. If he wasn't aware of that fact, he's obviously been tricked."

"Maybe you have a reason for saying that, but . . ." That was Gorobe Toda speaking. "Which part is wrong? Or is it wrong from beginning to end?"

"No, I wouldn't say that. Generally speaking, it's reasonable enough. But the important parts have been altered, and it's done in such a way that we can't make a distinction if we put them together. For example, this part and this one are obvious deceptions. It's far from the Great Bear, but they're the ones we trust the most in Edo."

"Are you really sure?" Kyunosuke's voice was harsh. "If that's true, it will become important."

"I'm absolutely positive. We've got to check up on this Okumura fellow as soon as possible. Even if he isn't a spy, we've got to assume that they know what we're up to, since we've been tricked like this."

"I think you're going too far. If that were the case, we'd have heard from Ohara," Toda said, in an effort to ease the tension. "You're constantly in contact with him, aren't you, Kugata?"

"Yes. But Ohara is that kind of person, so . . ."

"No, I'm not going too far," said the high-pitched voice. "Anyway, we've got to check up on Okumura. Maybe we've missed our chance."

The man speaking in the high-pitched voice was Samanosuke Watanabe, who had arrived that day from the Edo mansion to announce Lord Toda's proposed return to Ogaki in October and to visit Kugata after nightfall. Of course Ichi was not aware of this and she could not understand the major import of the conversation, but their remarks about her brother and the *Seishukufu* astounded her.

My brother Bennosuke has some connection with those people. He's doing the same work they are. And for some reason they're going to investigate him because he's done something unfavorable to them. The thoughts whirled in her confused brain.

The conversation grew lower. Soon she heard someone leaving. Ichi slid back into bed and closed her eyes. Her time was approaching, and she was greatly affected by heat. The perspiration seemed to pour out of her body even if she lay still, and if she lay in the same position for any length of time her lower body would become numb. The child's movements were growing stronger, and since it would suddenly kick her while she was dozing she often cried out in her sleep. These things alone would have been enough to disturb her, but her added worry about the frightening things happening one after the other wore her out mentally and physically.

If I'm completely worn out it will have a bad effect on the child. My husband says he's almost certain nothing will happen, and all my worry can't help him, so I shouldn't think about it any more. My duty as a woman is to give birth to a dear, healthy, good child. This line of thought finally soothed her into a deep sleep.

She was suddenly awakened by a touch on her shoulder, and found her husband squatting outside the mosquito netting.

"What happened?" he asked. "Are you awake now? . . . You were being tormented by a nightmare, so I woke you up. Did you have a bad dream?"

"Not that I know of." Ichi straightened the neckband of her kimono and sat up. "Had you already gone to bed?"

"I'm going now. I bet you'd like to wipe the perspiration off. Shall I cool the towel?"

"I perspire so much." Picking up the towel from the head of the bed, Ichi wiped her breast. "Won't the gods punish me for allowing my husband to do such a thing?"

"The hardship of giving birth will balance it."

Ichi closed her eyes as she sat back in the bed. She heard the sound of water being drawn from the well, and it made her feel like a baby being tenderly cared for. This was the first time Shinzo had done such a thing for her. While she did not view it as the expression of a special love, still she was pleased by his kind treatment of her at this lonely midnight hour.

Shinzo had returned to the mosquito netting.

"After you've dried yourself you'd better lie down. I'll fan you a little." He picked up the fan from the head of the bed. "Ichi, you've grown thinner."

"Have I really? I have the impression I'm gaining weight, and I feel uneasy."

"First of all there's this heat. Then you worry all the time. But since everything you eat is taken by the baby, maybe there's nothing to be done about it."

"To be a woman is to be useless." Ichi turned aside for a moment. "They say that husband and wife are two acting as one, but all I can do is get upset and worry as I watch my husband suffering for his important work. I can't understand a thing about it, and I can't even help you. No wonder we women and children are lumped together into one group! But when all is said and done, are we women really as helpless as that?"

"You're wrong. Husband and wife are two acting as one, but that doesn't mean they're the same. The fact is that if telling his wife something will only make her worry, the husband shouldn't tell her. Not because he considers her a helpless thing, but rather out of love, I think. A woman is by no means useless. She's to be treated kindly and protected."

"But don't you think such concern springs from the idea that women are powerless and undependable?"

"Then let me ask you this," said Shinzo, trying to be cheerful. "I do nothing but worry every time I think about your coming confinement. You'll probably get through it safely, but what are you going to do if it's difficult? No matter how much this worry is at the back of my mind, I am in the end helpless, for I can't share the pain of delivery with you. In this case, do you think I'm not a person you can depend on?"

"You're changing the subject. You know very well that I'm not asking you about that."

"Let's stop talking like this—if we go on much longer, we'll find that even the idea of husband and wife being two acting as one isn't true. Ultimately everyone is alone. . . . But talking about it doesn't help at all. In fact," said Shinzo in a lighter tone of voice, "I have a favor to ask you. If you open the left-hand door of the closet in my room, you'll find a bundle at the far end. You can feel it with your hand, even when the room is pitch black. This bundle is very important. If something happens while I'm out of the house, I want you to take care of it."

"What do you mean by taking care of it?" Ichi asked. She began to tremble.

"I want you to hide this bundle as best you can in a completely safe place. This is the main consideration, it must be absolutely safe. I want you to take care of this no matter what happens. Do you understand?"

Ichi nodded wordlessly.

"I don't think the occasion will arise, but since there's always the chance that worse will come to worst, I'm asking you to do this for me. I don't want my mother to worry, and Tatsuya's too easygoing. . . . Why don't you lie down now?"

"I'm just fine now, so please go to bed. I'm overwhelmed by your kindness."

"I'm not doing it just for you, Ichi, so don't let it overwhelm you. Just lie down. . . . To be honest, maybe I'm doing it for the baby you're carrying. I'm also a father, you know."

His kindness just isn't natural, Ichi thought as she lay down. Something serious is going on. Since he can't talk about it, he's being very careful. "Take care of the bundle in the closet. . . . We'll find that even the idea of husband and wife being two acting as one isn't true. Ultimately everyone is alone." . . . This house and the life at this home will be ended. Everything must come to an end.

Ichi began to sob quietly. Shinzo, silent now, continued to move the fan noiselessly.

7

AFTER the departure of Shinzo and Kyunosuke for work the following morning, Chusai Yonezawa's wife came to the house to examine Ichi. She was a squint-eyed woman with a cheerful personality, but people pitied her because of her extreme obesity.

"Since I don't have children, I keep cats," she used to explain, by way of introduction to her incessant conversations about cats. "I have more than ten now. Whenever I meet someone I urge him or her to take one of my cats, but still they keep multiplying, and I don't know what to do. But they're so lovable. . . ."

She was encouraging about Ichi's condition. "You're taking such good care of yourself and are doing so well that I can't find anything wrong," she said, narrowing her eyes and wiping her forehead. "There's absolutely nothing wrong, but you might give birth ahead of schedule. I'm sure I told you it would be September 4th. Hmm . . . I still can't tell exactly, but please be prepared for a slightly earlier date. No, no, you needn't worry; the baby is growing well."

Ichi had been thinking that the continual lack of sleep and her extreme nervousness must be having a bad effect on her body. So the news that the date might be moved up, rather than the assurance that she was doing well, stuck in her mind, and her heart sank as she thought this was just what she had feared.

An unusually cool wind was blowing, and the trees in the garden and the bamboo and bushes in the back yard rustled in the breeze. Ichi was now feeling the lack of sleep of the preceding night; her nerves were rubbed raw and she had no energy to do anything.

After lunch she went to her room. The wind blowing in through the window was so pleasant that it almost intoxicated her. She put up a small screen with a bush-clover design and lay down for a moment. She had no intention of going to sleep, but the fatigue accumulated in her body must have suddenly overwhelmed her. She fell so soundly asleep that although she realized someone was in the room and was trying to awaken her, she was unable to answer immediately.

"Sister! Sister!" The person called her several times.

She finally awoke with a start. Kyunosuke's wild eyes and totally white face were surprisingly close to hers. He was covered with so much perspiration that he seemed to be dripping water, and his shoulders were heaving from his heavy breathing.

"Sister, please don't be shocked." Kyunosuke licked his dry lips. "There's been some misunderstanding, and I want you to leave the house. Please get your belongings together—only what's absolutely necessary, because we've got to hurry."

"My husband . . ." Ichi felt dizzy as she stood up. "What's happened to my husband? Is he safe?"

"I'll explain it to you later. Please get ready first. Mother is coming now."

Ichi saw that Kyunosuke's *hakama* had a foot-long tear up the side, a tear unmistakably made by a sword. He ran out of the room. Ichi's knees were trembling, and for just a moment everything went black around her. Perhaps it was only an illusion, but in this pitch-dark space she could see her husband's smiling face so clearly, more vivid than reality, and so fresh that she even thought she could touch him.

My husband has died. Her instinctive feeling was

definite, not vague, and so strong that it left no room
for doubt. An unexpected change occurred in her
mind with the coming of this feeling, an awareness of
the fact that her husband's death was a natural event
and had been destined to happen in this way from the
beginning, that everything which had happened until
now had been a promise pointing toward the accom-
plishment of that event. This feeling came floating up
to the surface of her consciousness, and despite its
brief existence it provided a balance for Ichi's emo-
tions by encouraging determined action. This intuition
of her greatest possible misfortune, namely, her
husband's death, aroused power and courage in her.

She began to hear the wind rustling through the
bamboo bush in the back yard. Although her legs were
still trembling, her head and eyes were wide awake,
and she felt strangely calm. She looked around the
room, then put away the screen, mumbling, "This
object, that one . . ."

Her mother-in-law was running down the corridor.
Ichi went into her husband's bedroom, exclaiming
"Oh!" and remembering what she had forgotten.

"Ichi! Ichi! Where are you?"

"Here." Ichi took her husband's bundle out of the
closet. "I'm coming, mother."

If I have to leave here, there's no place to hide
this. It's not heavy or large, so I should take it with
me, Ichi thought, holding the bundle to her breast.
Only last night my husband asked me to take care of
it. It was after midnight, and that's not so many hours

ago. He mustn't have expected the crash to come so quickly. But maybe he had an inkling of it. Then how did he feel when he moistened the towel and fanned me without saying anything after I started to cry?

As Ichi's thoughts ran on, her heart filled with emotion for the first time, and her tears poured down. "Darling!" she murmured, and pressed the bundle to her face.

What happened between then and their departure from the house was confused. Everything happened at once and in total disorder, so that afterwards she could not distinguish before from after. What remained in her memory were the vigorous activity of Kyunosuke, who was running in every direction through the house, the calm voice of Iso giving orders to the servants, and the appearance of Tatsuya as he stood absentmindedly in a corridor holding a sack containing a creel and his favorite fishing rod. Somehow he had managed to get hold of them. He looked like a child who had been taken away from his playground and did not know what to do, and his nonchalant, easygoing appearance was totally at odds with the urgent atmosphere of that moment.

Ichi could not even be sure at what point the officers had come from the castle. Perhaps it was after she had finished packing her belongings. Or, since Kyunosuke was standing next to her and scolding, "You can't carry so much. Can't you cut it down to half that?" it might have been before she had finished.

In any event, there was a shout from the front room,

and Kyunosuke and Gorobe Toda ran in that direction, their swords in their hands. Ichi remembered that the servant girl began to cry, that Iso took the Buddhist mortuary tablets of the family ancestors out of the household altar, that she heard a sound like that of a clothes pole falling down, that a male servant named Wakichi could not untie the string of his basket and was upset. Ichi wanted to take as many valuable things from her bridal trousseau as she could, and even made two extra bundles, thinking it would be all right if she carried them herself.

These things seemed to happen after the fighting had started in the garden. Yet again it seemed as if packing was the first thing she had done, she was not at all sure. She heard the words, "By order of the lord—don't resist," and Kyunosuke's answer, "I shan't resist, please wait for us, we're getting ready." Was it after this or at the same time that three strange samurai came into the garden yelling something in a high-pitched shout uttered in a shivering trance, as if they themselves were frightened to death?

Human feelings are strange. Ichi remembered very vividly that a honeybee was buzzing aimlessly about the room just then, that Gorobe Toda said, "I'll take care of this!" while Kyunosuke exclaimed, "Brother! Everything's all right here! Take care of the others!" and that then a sword flashed in the garden. She picked up the two bundles and started out the back door, but turned in time to see Kyunosuke shouting and whirling his sword.

Wakichi, carrying some bundles in his basket, Nihei, an elderly male servant, and the servant girl went with them. She disappeared along the road, and they parted from Nihei at the bank of the Ibi River. (Ichi later learned that Kyunosuke had made sure they would not take anyone except Wakichi and had told them to leave Wakichi, too, at an appropriate place, so that he would not know where they were going.)

When they parted from Nihei, Tatsuya took the servant's bundles. Until then Ichi had not noticed that Tatsuya was with them. She remembered his holding the fishing rod and basket and standing absent-mindedly in the corridor, but she had no recollection whatsoever of his activity after that. When she saw him taking the bundles from the servant, his presence there came as a complete surprise, almost a shock, to her.

"You see where the willows are growing thickly, mother?" Tatsuya asked. The four of them continued along the bank for another twenty yards. Then Tatsuya pointed to a section of the river, saying, "Quite often we catch big catfish there."

"Catfish are disgusting." Iso made a face and shook her head. "The very name makes me shudder. Catfish . . . have you ever fished for them, Tatsuya?"

"I think it was last year that I came home with a cut hand, wasn't it? It was cut by a catfish. Those fellows have a hooklike thing at their chins, and people say even professional fishermen can be injured by it if they're not careful."

Ichi listened to this conversation in utter amazement. Were these people really that insensitive? She even wondered if they were lacking something mentally. Soon she was attacked by a fit of anger that left her feeling almost dizzy, and she halted on the road. After continuing for about eight yards, Iso and Tatsuya discovered that she had stopped walking. They turned, and her mother-in-law came back.

"What's happened to you? Aren't you feeling well?"

"I'm all right."

"Please bear with it for just a little while longer," Tatsuya called from where he was standing. "A little further on we'll come to a shady place where you can rest comfortably as long as you like. So please continue walking a little longer."

8

 A LARGE peaked cloud glared blindingly down from its position over the Yoro mountain chain to the west. Wherever the travelers looked they saw only continuous stretches of green fields or moors thick with cattails and lotus. Here and there amid the green foliage they could see farmhouses surrounded by trees to protect them from flood damage.

Since it was midday, there was no sign of a human presence in the fields, not even a child playing in the river. The wind was still blowing along the river bank, but when they went out onto the road they were surrounded by an unbearably humid heat rising from the grass and the steaming water in the rice paddies. They walked along the road for two hours, turning to the right or the left, enjoying some rest whenever they found a clump of trees.

After passing through many small villages, they finally reached Kawado, beside the Ibi River. It was a landing stage for boats going to Kuwana in Ise, and despite the lack of houses it was a respectable-looking post town, with two or three inns that served lunch. The group entered one inn which looked a little better than the others, washed their feet, loosened their kimonos, and dried off.

Here they parted from Wakichi. "Since we're going down to Kuwana by boat," Iso lied, "you may go home now. I think we'll come back to Ogaki some-day, and when we do I'll get in touch with you and ask you to come back to work for us." Then she wrapped up some money and gave it to him.

Wakichi insisted that he wanted to see them off on the boat, if he was not allowed to accompany them as far as Kuwana. But Iso talked him out of it, saying that this would attract attention, and sent him away after allowing him to eat lunch and drink some saké.

The three of them rested until the sun began to sink in the west. They left some of their belongings with the innkeeper and headed back toward the Ibi River.

Where in the world are we going? Ichi wondered. Tatsuya and Iso had told her nothing. It was the season of shortening days, and the sky had begun to turn a dark, madder red while the evening wind blew over the fields. The Yoro mountain chain had turned dark purple, and the foothills were already hidden by a thick mist. "Jhat, jhat, jhat," the wind rustled over the rice fields that surrounded them as far as they could see. The songs of clear-toned cicadas came to their ears from a great distance, and the lotus flowers glowed on the dim moor. The scene gave Ichi, who was walking without even knowing where she was going, an incomparably lonely, helpless feeling.

"You know, over there you can see where the streams of the river meet, sister." Tatsuya, who was covered with perspiration from carrying the bundles, looked at Ichi as they climbed up the river bank. "Just a little lower down lies the country of the Matsudaira, lords of Takasu. Since Ogasa village is right near the border, it's said to be very convenient in emergencies."

"Is that where we're going?" Ichi asked.

"Of course." He looked puzzled. "Kyunosuke told you that, didn't he? Didn't you hear him?"

"Nobody heard it—you're the only one who knew it," said Iso. "Some friend lives in this what's-its-name village?"

"You really are careless, mother. The old man's house is there. You should be a little more alert at such a time."

"How could I know something I don't know? How on earth is some old man connected with Kyunosuke? Is he a friend of yours too?"

"I think it's Josuke," Ichi contributed, "the farmer who's always carrying vegetables."

"Since you don't have practical common sense, you don't even notice such things, mother. Let's go down that way, sister. That hut is a ferry house."

When they climbed down the river bank they found a field of reeds, as tall as a man, through which a narrow, damp alley led toward the river. It was already dark among the thick reeds, and only the tops of the leaves, swayed by the wind, caught the light.

Since she could not bear the feeling of water penetrating the straw sandals tied to her feet, Ichi tried as much as possible to walk in areas covered by the roots of the reeds. Suddenly she was startled by a strange, momentary pain in her stomach. At Kawado she had felt a slight pain, but she attributed it then to a cold caught after perspiring a lot along the long road. Since it had stopped immediately without really hurting her, she had not paid it too much attention. But this time the strange new pain was ghastly, and it sent a splitting ache through her entire body.

The baby may be coming, she thought, as she remembered that the scheduled date might be moved up. She groaned, wondering what she would do if the worst happened in this place, and she trembled all over, as if shaken by a chill. By the time she reached the ferry the pain had ceased, but upon reflection she realized that she had not felt the baby move for a long time. Having heard that just before birth the baby would not move, she thought there was no mistaking it. As soon as she walked into the ferryman's hut she told Iso about the pain, for she could no longer bear to keep it to herself.

"I don't think it's possible," her mother-in-law said, but even she turned pale. "It's just a little over seven months, isn't it? Don't you think both today's events and this long walk are making you feel a little bit ill?"

"I hope that's what it is . . . but is Ogasa village very far away?"

Iso left the hut, calling "Tatsuya! Tatsuya!" As the ferry boat had just crossed over to the other side, Tatsuya had gone to the river to call it back.

Iso soon returned and told Ichi in a relieved tone of voice that the village was only a bit less than a mile beyond the boat landing.

"If that's all it is," Iso said, "it's only a step. There's a long time between pains in the first birth, so even if your time has come you'll be all right until you get there. . . . And now, Ichi, you shouldn't think about anything else except giving birth. This alone is your job. Be brave and forget about everything else but that. All right?"

"Mother." Ichi looked into her mother-in-law's

eyes. "Have you given up hope too, mother? My husband is already . . ."

"I'm not giving up hope or anything else," Iso quietly interrupted her. "Since self-sacrifice is required for the performance of a samurai's duty, it's enough that he does not disgrace the name of our ancestors and stray from the *bushido*.* I believe he certainly did his duty."

Iso's voice was quiet, and there was nothing artificial in her expression. She said exactly what she was thinking, and her quiet words penetrated Ichi's mind. Only a short time ago, while walking along the riverbank, she had listened to Iso's and Tatsuya's conversation and been angered by their seeming insensitivity. She had even wondered how they could talk about such carefree things in such unfortunate circumstances and whether there was something mentally defective in them. Now for the first time she knew how wrong she had been. She could now remember her flurried and confused condition and the upheaval caused in her by her attachment to her husband. She realized that she was the one who should be laughed at. She bowed her head and held her lips tight in quiet determination.

I shall become stronger. My husband has died to fulfill his duty as a samurai. He sacrificed his own life

---

* *Bushido*: originally the purely military code of the samurai, stressing unquestioning loyalty and obedience and placing honor above life. In the eighteenth century it gradually evolved into a set of moral rules which spread through every social class.

for the Ogaki clan without the slightest hesitation. I am the wife of such a brave man.

In the boat she had the second labor pain. It was weaker than the first one, and Ichi's mind was strangely calm. She watched the river waves, which were turning a wintry color, and became even calmer as she thought. I shall give birth to a child, even if my time comes in the fields. Since mother, who has given birth to three children, is with me, and Tatsuya, I shouldn't worry about anything.

The scenery changed completely on the other side of the river. Perhaps because this was high ground, it showed less flood damage; there were more trees, and the hamlet of farmhouses was larger and serene looking. It was already dusk, and people were returning from the fields, walking along the street, laughing and talking in loud voices. The smoke of cooking fires rose with melancholy peacefulness from the tree-shrouded houses.

These people have no worries, Ichi thought. They go home after their day's work is finished, they take a bath, wash off their sweat and fatigue, and then the whole family gathers around a peaceful dinner table. They are concerned with nothing but their fields and families; they live humbly and are satisfied to support their loved ones.

For a moment Ichi was tempted to compare their lives with her own present circumstances, but she shook her head energetically and continued her heavy walk. Tatsuya apparently had been here several times.

He led the way through a narrow alley surrounding a mulberry field and went behind a stable. They reached their destination sooner than they had expected.

Later Ichi realized that they had approached the house from the rear. Branches bearing large quantities of already ripe persimmons barred their passage. They crept under the branches, which crisscrossed so low that without proper caution they might have bumped their heads. An old man was standing in the bare black garden and looking in their direction.

At that point Ichi was attacked by the third severe labor pain, but she nevertheless recognized the old man Josuke. Later she had no clear recollection of what kind of conversation they had exchanged with him or of how she had gotten into the house. The pain, which had started from somewhere in the center of her stomach, spread up and down with a severity that almost ripped her body apart, and her abdomen was squeezed with the wave of an acute pain. She tried unsuccessfully to suppress the moan coming through her clenched teeth. She crouched, but someone picked her up, and she was unable even to say that she could walk by herself.

Sometime after midnight, with the help of Josuke's wife, Gen, Ichi gave birth to a baby girl.

9

 ICHI'S idea that Josuke looked more like a retired elderly townsman than a farmer was correct—he was one of the rich landowners of Ogasa village. This was only a retreat for him; his real home was in Honaza. Rumor had it that long ago his family had had the family name* Washizu and that they had seen better days.

An excerpt from the Heiji Story, handed down from generation to generation, had this to say about Josuke's family name:

> Thus Yoshitomo had been staying with Ohi. But since things were going that way, he summoned Kamata, who was to leave shortly, and told him of his idea that he should get to the Inland Sea, since he could hardly go by the open sea route. Then Kamata answered that a man named Kuro-mitsu Washizu was a younger brother of Ohi and

---

* In old Japan, only samurai families and a few merchants and farmers who had performed distinctive service for their lords were permitted to have family names. Most farmers were known only by their given names. If someone once had had a family name, it was therefore an indication that he came from a distinguished family.

that since he was a notorious thief and a cou-
rageous man regarded with some honor, why not
travel with him.

Ichi had once read the story.

In addition to his 7,500 acres of land and large tract
of forest, Josuke owned a magnificent home and five
storehouses, built in a farmhouse style that gave no
hint of power or prestige. Old Josuke seemed to dislike the family legend, and smilingly said that "It's all
invented—one of my ancestors who suddenly acquired
the status of a small landowner made it up to gain
prestige." Not even one generation was missing from
his 800-year-old family genealogy, and this made it
untrustworthy even in the eyes of the general public.

Monshichi, the head of the family, had three
children. He had put his fields and forests into the
hands of an overseer and spent his life collecting old
manuscripts and writing *haiku*. As for Josuke, he felt
that it was a waste to be idle after retirement, so he
carried the fruits of the seasons—his homegrown
vegetables, persimmons, and pears—to Ogaki several
days a week, thereby earning some additional money.
Josuke and the head of the family obviously did not
get along well, and apparently they hardly ever saw
each other.

It was well known that Josuke's wife, Gen, would
not concern herself with the fields or household
matters. She was constantly being asked to deliver a
child or go to homes where there was a difficult case

of illness. Her talents along these lines seemed to be quite famous, and sometimes she would even be called on to spend the night with some family of the Takasu clan, whose lords were the Matsudaira family. She was rumored to be fifty-seven, the same age as Josuke, but with her thick black hair and shining, ruddy cheeks she looked ten years younger. She was not talkative, but had a brisk manner and a vivacious, girlish laugh.

"Don't think I'm boasting," she would often say, "but I flatter myself that I'm second to none in delivering a child. By now I've delivered a lot of children successfully; for example, a breech birth when even the doctor had given up hope. I think the trick is that I put myself into the frame of mind of the woman giving birth. But maybe nature has given me some special talent."

She also said that cures were accidental and that it was not true that she knew medicine or performed spells. Whenever she heard that a sick person had been despaired of by his doctor, she could not stay home— she had to visit the patient uninvited and console him.

"Nobody wants to die—that's human nature," she would say. "But all human beings must die sooner or later—shogun or beggar, they'll all go. Even the Buddha died. So if a person's illness is destined to be cured, he'll be cured even if a doctor despairs. Or someone who's fit as a fiddle in the morning will die by drowning in a river. We have to leave our natural span of life to nature. . . . All these things I say to the patient during the two or three days I spend with him. Somebody said my talk is more relaxing than a sermon by a Buddhist priest. I just want the patient to die with a relieved and tranquil mind, but since his sickness is sometimes cured . . ." And she would laugh.

This behavior by retired people who had at least a tradition of descent from So-and-so Washizu (even if it was difficult to take the tradition seriously) and who were major landowners was apt to become a source of gossip. However, in the case of this couple there was no gossip, and in fact many people admired them and depended more on them than on their own parents. Even people from other villages took off their hats in greeting when they met Josuke and Gen. This could have been due to Josuke's family connections or to the fact that Gen would never accept anything for giving help. But Ichi soon realized that when all was said and done their popularity depended on their personalities.

The saying was that a baby one month premature would not live to grow up. But Gen told Ichi confidently, "I'm positive your baby will grow up. You know, a child even two months premature will survive, even if it's abandoned. So there's no reason why a baby a little less than two months premature won't. And since she's so strong, you have nothing to worry about."

It was true that the baby was strong for a premature baby. The wet nurse's milk must have been generous, because by the time the frost began to settle the child had become surprisingly plump and was growing so well that nobody would guess she had been premature.

Ichi's milk had flowed poorly from the very beginning. According to Gen, her mammary glands were not fully opened because her pregnancy had been cut short, but her milk would flow better as she let the baby suck. However, Ichi's glands did not open at all, perhaps because the baby's sucking power was not strong enough since she was getting milk from someone else; so the feeding of the baby was left to the nurse.

Ichi named the baby Nobu. After celebrating Nobu's name day—the seventh day in the life of a newborn child—Ichi watched the face of the infant sleeping beside her in the dim light of the coming dawn and cried for the sad thoughts filling her heart.

There were many sayings about the care of a child. One should never let it be buffeted about by a strong wind, one should take care of it as if it were a butterfly or a flower, one should bring it up "with a nurse and a parasol," as the expression went. Ichi had been brought up with the greatest care, as if all of these sayings had been applied to her. She had no recollection of ever having asked for anything because she had been given things constantly, some of which she had not even wanted or cared about. She had been loved, worried over, cared for, and spoiled by visitors, to say nothing of her parents and brothers.

Ichi compared her life with that of her child. What a poor child she is destined to be! she thought. Even while you were still in my body, Nobu, your mother passed days of uneasiness and suspicion. In addition to losing the most important final fifty days, when you should have been receiving the necessary equipment for your entrance into the world, you came into it in the shock of great misfortune and an excess of exhaustion which had befallen your mother, and in a room in a stranger's house.

Suppose my husband has died already (for even Iso seems to think he is gone). . . . From now on Nobu's future will not be an easy one. Actually, we are hunted people. We have to hide from the eyes of the Ogaki castle people. If this goes on for long, just staying alive will not be easy. . . . Nobu! What's going to become of you? Ichi looked at the baby's sleeping face and bit the edge of the bed cover in an effort to keep her endless sobbing from her mother-in-law's ears. Her dark depression lasted for ten days after the birth.

The room loaned to Ichi had formerly been Josuke's room. It had a square window with a southwesterly exposure, and along its east side was an open veranda with deep clay eaves. Beyond the veranda could be seen only a rather large, bare, muddy garden, and beyond that was a persimmon orchard through which green fields were visible. From the window she had a view of the Yoro mountain chain, which rose into the sky in such a way that it seemed to completely embrace the terraced, plowed land, the woods, and the hamlets.

Since childhood Ichi had always shed solitary tears

whenever she looked at mountains, for they aroused a sad and lonely feeling in her heart. The distant Mount Fuwa and Mount Yoro had been visible from the Okumura house in Ogaki, but she had made a determined youthful effort not to turn her eyes in their direction. This memory now returned to Ichi's mind after the long interval of so many years.

The mountain she saw from her bed was much lower, quite different from the one she had looked at in Ogaki. In the morning she could clearly make out its deep groves of trees, the slanting surface of miscanthus waving in the wind, and the paths zigzagging up the mountainside. The mountain received the direct rays of dawn and shone with a beautiful, refreshing blue green color. Ichi was almost unable to endure the scene between noon and dusk when the face of the mountain would blanch from the glare of the overhead sun. But soon after the sun passed behind the mountain chain, its furrows and valleys offered a very vivid picture of light and shadow contrasts, the lighted areas being very bright while the shadowy areas were as dark as if they had no substance. This lasted only for a very short while, but nothing sharpened Ichi's awareness of time quite as much as this moment-by-moment movement of the sun.

Oh, the miscanthus field has already become a shadow. The cedar grove over there is just as dark. Mumbling to herself, Ichi would wonder what sorrow or pleasure would make people go from laughter to tears in such a short time. She would never again be able to see that sunlight which until now had been shining on the miscanthus field; it was gone forever, and tomorrow's sunlight would be a completely different one. Human beings' sorrows and pleasures, even their lives, passed on and disappeared, just like this sun which was moving moment by moment. If everything passed away like this, were not all human actions a waste? Such thoughts persisted in her mind.

At dusk the mountain would change to dark blue, then to purple. Then it would sleep, as if it had become a dark shadowgraph in an evening mist which was rising from its foothills. At this time of day in particular, the contrast of the still bright evening sky with the darkness of the mountain's shadow stirred a vague sorrow in the viewer's mind. Ichi felt that the mountain was weeping out of pity for her.

"That's right, girl. I have seen thousands and millions of other people. Many lives and events have been repeated, yours among them. Your peaceful life, your pleasure and happy days are over. You will have to pass through dark, sad, difficult days, just as millions of other people have done. It is your destiny. Poor girl. All human beings are the same. Poor Ichi." The message blew through her heart like an elegy.

Of course, such dark thoughts did not last long. Ichi soon recovered her composure, and simultaneously her feelings of sorrow for the child she was watching turned to passionate love. The change occurred very suddenly in Ichi's mind and filled her completely. I must not lose this child. I will raise her happily. I will give her everything. Her love conquered the dark thoughts with surprising strength.

Nobu, you don't have a father, a house, or even property. But your mother will give you all these things. Since your mother has been too happy, she will devote the rest of her life to you. Dear Nobu, please grow up strong. Then I'll make you happy, happier than anyone else. And Ichi firmly believed that this was within her power.

During this period she learned a little about current conditions in Ogaki. Josuke went down to the castle town every three days to sell vegetables and collected rumors from some samurai households which patronized him. However, despite the old man's eager efforts, everything was hazy and vague with the exception of two or three points. Gorobe Toda had been slain on the road to Nakatsuji, the *roshoku* Geki Ohara had been confined to his house, several samurai and their families had been summoned before the public prosecutor, and a few of them had deserted and fled the clan after a fight.

As for the Kugata family, the rumors were contradictory. Some people said that the entire family was being detained by the public prosecutor. There was a rumor that Shinzo and Kyunosuke had been run down in the castle and slain. How much of this was true was not clear. One could only guess that the clan rulers were keeping everything, including the reason for the events, a secret.

The news that Kyunosuke had been slain in the

castle together with Shinzo had to be false, since he had returned home in his torn *hakama,* and there was only one chance in a million that they had returned to the castle afterwards. But if both were among those who had deserted the clan after a battle, Kyunosuke would have visited them long ago, since it was he who had advised the family to take refuge in this village. He might have been slain or caught while escaping. This was the only point which worried Ichi, but she would have to wait for time to clarify this point.

Ichi thought that all that she could do was wait for the future to clear up the story. All she wanted to know was the truth concerning the result her husband and the others had been trying to achieve. She knew from her husband's talk that it had something to do with politics, and she felt that she must at any price find out exactly what it was, what system they were fighting against, and what system would have been set up had her husband and the others overthrown the old one. She wanted to be able to tell Nobu about it one day when the child grew up.

She guessed that there was no use asking Iso about it. Despite Tatsuya's happy-go-lucky personality he was, after all, a man, and so perhaps he might have heard something. With this in mind, Ichi casually tried to worm a hint out of him, but he knew no more than Iso. He was so open in manner that he did not arouse in her even a suspicion that he might be hiding something. All he said was, "When the time comes, we'll be able to find out all about it. It's nothing to worry about."

Like Ichi, Tatsuya had been captivated by the baby as soon as it was born. Iso's fondness for the child was understandable, given that it was her first grandchild. But Tatsuya's love for the baby was rather out of the ordinary, and things often happened which made Ichi burst into laughter as she watched him. Only ten days after the baby's birth he began to sit beside Nobu and talk to her. Ichi told him that the baby could not see a thing, but he refused to believe it.

"I don't think that's possible. Sure she can see! Look, when I move, she looks in that direction, doesn't she?"

"That's called 'distinguishing objects.' It's just that her eyes are attracted by light and shadow."

"Maybe that's usually the case. But since Nobu was born ahead of time, she's getting wisdom ahead of time. Look—she's laughing, isn't she?"

So Tatsuya behaved, and if Ichi said nothing he would talk to the baby for hours. Gen had advised them not to hold her too much, but once it became safe to hold her (around the time when the frost began to settle) he wanted to hold her so often that Ichi had a difficult time refusing him, which she did with the remark that it would not be good if the baby got into the habit of being held. However, since Tatsuya began helping Josuke in the fields shortly thereafter, matters improved.

Long afterwards Ichi found out that Tatsuya had years earlier given up making a living as a samurai and had been thinking of becoming a farmer if the opportunity presented itself. It was with this hope in mind that he had stopped Josuke and chatted whenever the old man had shown up. The two of them had made some plans for Tatsuya to become a farmer, and Tatsuya said that he had often visited this place to study the land for that purpose.

Salvation by a coincidence is not so unusual in life. Tatsuya's acquaintance with Josuke might have been a complete coincidence, but thanks to this coincidence Ichi had been able to give birth to her child safely with Gen's help and the family had been able to slip through the fingers of Toneri Otaka's clique, even though this place was not very far from Ogaki. This coincidence was something so valuable that it could even be said that all the help they had received and all the subsequent events resulted from coming here.

However, Ichi did not yet understand Tatsuya's feelings, and she even felt relieved that now her child was bothered less. But Tatsuya would come to hold Nobu as soon as he returned from the fields, as if he did not want to waste even the time spent in washing his hands.

"Were you lonely, Nobu?" he would ask. "Hmm, hmm, so you were lonely, I know, I know." He would make eyes at her while he talked. "When does she start walking, sister? Would New Year's be a bit too early?"

"Much more than a 'bit' too early," Iso answered, dumbfounded. "She simply can't walk before her first birthday, even if she's capable of walking earlier."

"Maybe that's usually the case, but since Nobu was born fifty days ahead of time . . ."

"You're always saying that, Tatsuya, but actually it's the other way around," said Iso. "The rule is that a child born prematurely will be slow in growing. You've misunderstood the saying."

"Sure, maybe that's generally the case, but . . ."

"There's nothing 'generally' or anything else in these things. By the way, what are you holding to your chest? It's falling out."

At these words Tatsuya hurriedly pressed his hands to his chest, but something slipped from his hands and fell to the ground.

It was a small pair of woven straw sandals attached by red thongs to clogs.

* * *

Part Three

10

ICHI DID not begin going to Minojin House in Shimada village until February of the following year, although she had conceived the idea during the preceding fall.

One day, after Nobu's birth, she had seen wagons piled high with something that looked like grass. They passed the house at frequent intervals, and Ichi asked Gen what the grass was and where it was going. Gen's explanation was that it was *toshin,* or wick grass. Most grass, she continued, was made up into the straw mats called *tatami,* but *toshin* was used by the workers at Minojin House to make flower mats, straw mats into which designs were woven with dyed rushes. The work required a special weaving machine, technique, and materials, and it was not easy to do. A flower mat was regarded as an unusual and expensive object.

Ichi herself had seen such a mat once, at the home of the *roshoku* Iki Toda. It had been about the size of two *tatami,* with a border of interwoven swastika patterns and a center motif of leaves and a peony-like flower. She remembered that its lines were generally crude and inaccurate, and she had not regarded it as beautiful.

"We could earn some money if we wove this kind of thing," Gen said. "But it's a job which requires patience, and some people are good at it while others aren't. Some people from this village are hired to work at Minojin House, but they never stay long."

Gen spoke as if to herself, but Ichi took the words as a hint. For some time she had been thinking of earning her living at a suitable job. She could not entertain the hope that her husband was still alive, and even if the family was allowed to return to the Kugata home, Kyunosuke or Tatsuya would be the head of the household. Things would have been different if her child had been a boy, but since it was a girl the question of succession was practically cut and dried. Moreover, since her hope of returning to the clan was uncertain, the best thing would be to plan on earning her own living and to forget completely about other possibilities for the time being.

The difficult point was the question of whether Ichi, who had been brought up in a life of ease, would be able to support the family. But Ichi did not think it would be that difficult. Her father had often said that if a person sticks for ten years to a single thing he is determined to achieve, he usually succeeds at it. An example of this was the story of a samurai, Sawada, who was a vassal of the Okumura family.

Sawada had begun in middle age to learn painting, and after studying for ten years had finally succeeded and become a good painter. Soon he left the Okumura household and took up residence in Osaka, where he gradually became popular and was sought out by numbers of students. Finally he started a separate school in Kyoto which also served as his workshop.

This vassal was a dull-witted, stupid man who had been unable to write his own name well before the age of thirty. People could find in him no keen perception or dexterity for painting, and even after he had begun his studies nobody had dared to say for sure that he would be a success. All this had happened before Ichi's birth, and she had not known him during this period. But since he came every year from Osaka to present New Year's greetings to her parents, she had often seen the taciturn, courteous, fat old man since his success. The painting of the four seasons on the six-fold screen which Ichi had brought with her to the Kugata home was his work. Her father's remark had made a deep impression on Ichi, especially after she had become acquainted with the painter. That a man unable to write his own name had yet become a painter was quite rare, but it nevertheless seemed to Ichi that his example was one of the things supporting her in her determination.

Her mother-in-law expressed disapproval, and did not quickly give her consent, saying that Ichi should not have to go to such lengths. Tatsuya was quite unable to express an opinion. But Ichi explained her idea to them quietly, and begged a little, saying, "If I do this maybe my feeling of depression will lift." The presence of a wet nurse for Nobu—a great convenience and the strongest argument of all—was a help. When Iso approved, Ichi immediately asked Gen to act as a go-between to take her to Minojin House after New Year's.

Shimada was on the bank of the Makida River, about two and a half miles to the northwest, and it had a landing stage called Karasue. It was the departure and arrival point for boats plying between Kyoto, Osaka, and Edo via Kuwana, and although it had few houses it was a prosperous, lively place. Minojin House, the first house this side of the village, consisted of three separate buildings set on four acres of land fenced in with willow trees. The willows looked peculiar, but the external appearance and the interior of the buildings were even more eccentric. The main house was three stories high and had a thatched, mountainshaped roof. The two other buildings looked like large, long boxes to which roofs and windows had been added.

"It's a very strange-looking house." Ichi looked around for a while with a feeling of wonderment.

"The master of the house is really an eccentric person, and he built his house to suit his personality," Gen answered. "People say there are many disturbing things about his way of life." She was leading Ichi to the main house as she spoke.

A large number of thick lacquered pillars about

three feet square surrounded an unfloored area. Then
came a shiny black floor which resembled a two-
stepped platform and which extended as far as the
back room. Ichi and Gen passed through the *shoji**
near the entrance and into a 12-mat room with an
earthen hearth, apparently a conference room.

Here Ichi met the elderly chief manager, Mankichi,
and was shown around the workshop. This consisted
of the two box-like buildings, one of which was used
for dyeing the rushes while the other served as the
weaving room. The dyeing room was large—over a
thousand square feet—and was divided into two areas.
Bottles of dyes and chemicals stood on the ground, and
the partition above them served as the drying area. To
the left and right were clapboard walls about eighteen
inches thick, made of cryptomeria board. Through
the use of windlasses, each board could be moved into
an oblique position to leave open spaces through which
the wind could freely pass.

A large fireplace stood against the partition between
the dyeing and drying areas, and someone explained
that in the rainy season and in winter the mats could
be dried by the heat from the fire. At this moment an
old woman crouching in front of the fireplace was
poking at logs as big as her arms. It was explained that
the heat from the fireplace did not immediately pass
through the roof, but went through tubes under the
floor to warm the room and was then forced out

* *Shoji:* a lightweight sliding screen used as a divider.

through the walls. Crosspieces were installed at lintel height, and the dyed rushes were hung in closely packed rows. Ichi listened to the man's voice in the sour-sweet odor of drying grass and dyeing materials. She felt their hot dampness steaming up from the floor. Perspiration stood in beads on her forehead.

Five women were weaving mats in the weaving area in the other building. Twelve weaving machines stood on a spacious plank flooring, but only five were in operation, and the man said that the others were idle because weavers could not be found. Two of the women were young, another was only a teenager, while the other two were middle-aged married women. Only the young girl seemed to be absorbed in her work; the other four appeared to have no interest or eagerness. As Ichi turned to go after her inspection of the room, one of the middle-aged women raised her husky voice and began to sing:

> If the mountain is burned down,
> The mother bird will escape.
> There is nothing more precious
> Than her own life.

Ichi returned to the main house and was told over tea about wages, working hours, and holidays. Mankichi, having likely learned something about her life from Gen, treated her courteously and even seemed anxious for her to come to work there.

"For some reason we're in a stalemate," said the

elderly chief manager, who bore some resemblance to Josuke, "but we feel that with an effort we can make a comeback. Anyway, it's the kind of job that has good prospects."

He looked at Ichi as if wondering what she was thinking. His small face was old and withered; only his clear eyes radiated a kind of power.

There was a lifeless, stagnant atmosphere throughout the house. Ichi could even sense a kind of deterioration, and it gave her an unpleasant sensation. But inspiration had come to her as she looked at the types of goods being woven. She also felt she could not refuse Mankichi's request heartlessly. After thinking it over for three days, she decided to take the job.

The night before her first day of work, Josuke and his wife cooked the red rice used for celebrations and prepared sweetfish with rice jelly. But they also expressed the fear that perhaps it was poor breeding to celebrate the first day of work by a samurai's wife.

"Then you're really going to start weaving flower mats tomorrow, sister?" Tatsuya asked, smiling. "I'm working in the fields and you're weaving flower mats. A great sight, isn't it?"

"You're awful, Tatsuya. You shouldn't call such a thing a great sight. It's exactly the opposite," said Iso.

"Oh no, mother," said Ichi smiling. "I think it's exactly what Tatsuya says. Don't you think we can call it a great sight if Tatsuya becomes a fine farmer and I have a shop for weaving flower mats? I really do intend to become the owner of a weaving shop."

"It might be all right . . ." Iso mumbled, and lowered her eyes. The hand holding the chopsticks seemed to tremble—but perhaps that was just Ichi's imagination.

Ichi could guess approximately what her mother-in-law was thinking. The samurai customs and the honor of the Kugata family name were deeply rooted in Iso's mind, and even now she hesitated to do things considered out of bounds.

If her life up to now has been her real life, it's really difficult and painful for her to leave it. If I were a little older, I might not be able to give it up so easily either. Ichi sympathized with her mother-in-law and realized that she herself must be cheerful and brave to change the older woman's way of thinking.

Then her new life began.

ICHI'S confused, restless life, exacerbated by her difficulties in getting used to the weaving machine, continued into spring. She tired easily and found it difficult to put up with the unpleasantness generated by her lack of harmony with the other weavers.

Since four more weavers had joined the group after Ichi, the unfriendly situation in the workroom was gradually improving. But two of the original employees—the woman who had sung the song and another housewife who seemed to be her best friend—constantly directed nasty looks toward Ichi and never hesitated to be mean to her or backbite her within earshot. There was no real reason for their behavior, only their resentment of Ichi's samurai background and the kindness shown to her by the owner, Teijiro, and old Mankichi. Ichi felt they would come around with time. In contrast, her problem with the owner would only grow worse.

One of the reasons for Ichi's decision to become a weaver was her desire to make a patterned flower mat of a new type. The products she had seen on her first visit differed little from the one she had seen in Iki Toda's house. Ichi wanted more designs in her work and more intricate beauty of both pattern and weaving.

About a month after her arrival she spoke of her desire to Mankichi and worked on patterns of her own design. Mankichi told the owner and then informed Ichi that Teijiro wanted her to concentrate exclusively on this job. But since she had no idea of what the result would be, and out of consideration for the other women's feelings, she decided that for the time being she would work on her mat at another machine for only two hours every afternoon.

One rainy March day, when the mountains and

fields were hidden in the mist of dancing rain drops, Ichi walked through the Minojin House gate and headed for the weaving room. She inclined her umbrella slightly and glanced at a person standing in front of the main house.

"Oh!" she cried. A shudder rose from the soles of her feet through her body, and she almost stopped breathing.

It was her husband.

A purple light sparked before her eyes. Ichi started to run toward him but went down on one knee. As she staggered forward, throwing aside her umbrella, the man began running toward her.

"What's the matter?" He took Ichi's hand and helped her up. Of course it was not Shinzo. In fact, the man bore no resemblance whatsoever to her husband. It was Teijiro, the owner of Minojin House.

"Did you stumble? Are you hurt?" Teijiro picked up her umbrella. A person of about thirty-five, he was thin, pale, and sad-looking, and Ichi was struck by his look of exhaustion and his extremely long, thin fingers.

Why did I mistake him for my husband? she wondered. He bore not the faintest resemblance to Shinzo, but when she closed her eyes the man she saw standing in front of the main house was not Teijiro but Shinzo. The powerful impression which had overwhelmed her at that moment remained with her for some time. Her heart beat faster, a strange feeling of paralysis overcame her from time to time, and she spent the entire day in the grip of a restless, uneasy feeling.

A few days after this incident Mankichi came to tell her that the master wanted to talk with her.

Ichi's heart beat fast. In answer to her question why, Mankichi said that Teijiro wanted to ask her about the work. Since she could think of no pretext for refusing, she went with Mankichi to the main house.

They entered the unfloored area of the house, the area Ichi had glimpsed on her first visit. Mankichi pushed open a *shoji* at the back of the room, and they went into a large central hall which contained a stairway.

So far the house had looked like any ordinary house which had sheltered many generations. But as they went up the stairs, the building's appearance and decor became quite unfamiliar. The broad staircase had a red handrail which shone brightly in the dim light, and instead of climbing up straight it zigzagged in three flights. On the walls of the two landings were splendid woven hangings. The one on the lower landing depicted strange flowers, birds, plants, and trees, while the other showed a young man in armor standing among flowering trees and holding a naked woman with one hand and the bridle of a horse with the other. The hanging was dark and sooty in color, and only the woman's body with its full breasts and curving hips was white and vivid. She was resting one hand on the young man's shoulder and hiding her mouth with an air of embarrassment behind the other hand. Ichi felt a burning sensation in her cheeks and a quickening of her heartbeat as she looked at the bright flesh, and she turned her head away.

At the top of the stairs they found themselves in a hallway containing at one end a solid-looking, sliding oak door; to its left was a high latticed window with an oiled-paper sliding sash, and to its right the wall, which looked like the back of a Buddhist altar at a temple.

Mankichi announced them before the sliding door, then opened it quietly and motioned Ichi to enter. She hesitated for a moment. Everything was alien and ostentatiously heavy, and a feeling akin to uneasiness came over her, a kind of premonition that she should not enter. But the owner, Teijiro, came out at that moment and, averting his eyes, invited her to come in. Ichi entered the room, walking as if in a trance. She heard the heavy sound of the sliding door closing behind her.

The walls of the room, which was about 20-mats long, were covered with striped and printed chintz, and a bright red carpet covered the floor. Pots, vases, and bowls with unfamiliar shapes and decorative patterns stood in rows on the shelves of a large and sturdy chestnut cupboard, while from inside a few glass saké cups with long stems gleamed darkly. Foreign books with strange bindings and designs lined the two lower shelves of a five-shelf bookcase about twelve feet long. On top of the bookcase stood an unglazed, colored pottery doll. Every piece of furniture—the high desk surrounded by low, deep inclining chairs, the bronze desk lamp with its handle, three pictures hanging on the transom, the armchair at the north window—was an unusual piece of work unlike anything Ichi had ever seen.

"Please sit down." Teijiro, his eyes still averted, offered her a chair and sat down himself. "Please feel at home. You needn't be reserved. . . . Please."

"What did you want to see me about? Since I'm at work now . . ."

"In fact it has to do with your work . . ." he began. He scowled for a moment, then twisted his lips as if in pain. "Mankichi talked to me about it the other day, and I gave instructions that you should experiment a little. As for the new mat you're working on now, I saw the one you're weaving and the ones you spoiled and threw away. That's when I decided to have a talk with you. What is your plan?"

"The patterns of the average mat use straight lines," Ichi began, "like squares sewn together, or swastikas. What's more, the flowers and leaves are crude and their colors are simple. I feel they lack variety, and I'd like to weave patterns with curved lines and complicated designs like flowers and birds, and to use more colors."

"I hear you're using rushes for the vertical lines also."

"Yes. I think I can weave vertical and horizontal patterns, like a crest pattern, a checkerboard, or a basket weave."

"A mat," said Teijiro after a short pause, during which he crossed his long fingers, "is only a carpet, a luxury item. It will never become a work of art, no matter how exquisite you make it. But even if it is only a carpet, naturally it's better if it's beautiful rather than merely useful. You saw the Gobelin tapestry on the staircase, didn't you?"

"Yes, I did." Ichi lowered her eyes. "It's the first time in my life I've seen such a thing, and I was astonished; it's so unusual and beautiful."

"It came from Holland, and it's only a wall hanging. But don't you think there's a difference between the way of life which produces and uses such an object, and the way of life which doesn't? . . . There are many ways of life. It's not just a difference of race or country; even here the style of living differs depending on wealth or poverty, circumstances, likes and dislikes. But it's true that our way of life is generally dark, modest, and lacking in variety. Don't you think so?"

Teijiro spoke eagerly. His pale face was becoming pink, and his eyes brighter.

"You must have found the style of this room eccentric," he continued. "Some objects have been handed down for generations in my family; others I took pains to buy. Some of them are even prohibited. Why did I collect these things, and why did I design such an eccentric interior? In a word, it's because I want to live a life of satisfaction. Man has five senses: sight, hearing, taste, touch, and smell. How he satisfies these senses shows how he lives. And this satisfaction must be as beautiful, keen, sweet, and intoxicating as possible. If he leaves only one of the senses idle, he cannot be called alive. . . . Everyone must die some-day. Even if a person builds a beautiful palace or amasses a fortune of millions or rises to a very honored position as minister or president, he will surely die someday, become a heap of bare bones, and decay under the tombstone. A thousand years from now everything will have disappeared. If this is so, a person must enjoy as much satisfaction as possible while still alive. He should not waste even a day or an hour; he should satisfy his five senses fully. Outside of this there is nothing of value. You can sacrifice everything to this goal. Everything!"

Teijiro suddenly turned pale and pressed his hands to his contorted face, as if seized with a fit. Ichi's hands were perspiring. A shudder like the shudder of temp-tation or danger one experiences upon looking into a deep gorge from the top of a cliff ran through her body.

Teijiro remained silent and motionless for some time. Finally he slowly took his hands away from his face and resumed speaking.

"I think that if you're going to make the flower mat you're thinking about, you should change the atmosphere of your life. To go back to the wall hang-ing on the stairs—first came the way of life which impelled people to weave it, and then it was made. I think that in order to produce a certain object one needs a way of life conducive to its production. I intend to advise you about this. If you want to go through with it, I'll help you as much as I can."

"Thank you very much," Ichi replied after a short silence. "But you don't know my personal history."

"Yes, I know the general outline. I meant it when I said I'd help you. I think there are many things which will be of use to you. Also, I think you'd better move in and live here, if you can, so that you'll have time to work."

Ichi involuntarily lowered her eyes, for the master's eyes looking at her that moment were very powerful, and again she felt a shudder beginning in her body. She told him that she would think it over and ask her mother-in-law, and left.

She paused when she reached the bottom of the stairs.

They're my husband's eyes. The powerful eyes of Teijiro gazing at me just now with their strong light are exact copies of my husband's eyes which gazed at me in the moonlight that night when I went after him and we embraced by the fence.

Now Ichi realized why she had mistaken Teijiro for her husband that rainy day.

She was unable to suppress a groan.

12

ICHI DID not tell her mother-in-law or Tatsuya about the incident. To Teijiro she behaved as if her answer was that she was not giving him any answer, and she went back and forth as usual between her house and the shop. Teijiro must have guessed what she was thinking and did not press her for a reply or refer to the subject. His indirect, casual kindnesses to her increased, but since they were concealed and had to do with the work, no one except the two housewives noticed. Inevitably, however, the situation was becoming a burden on Ichi's feelings.

The master was very solitary, sensitive, and, in a sense, weak; earlier in life he had been hurt deeply. Ichi learned that he had a wife and child, but his wife had returned to her parents' house three years ago, and it was said that they hardly saw each other. Mankichi said vaguely that "they couldn't get along." What the facts were Ichi could not guess, but she felt very sorry for Teijiro.

His solitary loneliness must have been the reason for his asking her to "move in here." She felt sorry for this unfortunate person, but on the other hand an instinctive feeling warned her to be careful with him because his passionate nature could not control the impulses of his sensitive, weak personality. Another factor was the strong temptation she experienced, a temptation as strong as her dislike of the way he had, there in the exotically decorated room, overwhelmed himself with his own cravings; equally detestable were his search for a purely sensual satisfaction and his suffering because such satisfaction was beyond his reach. His secret kindnesses, added to these dual feelings of sympathy and caution, set Ichi's nerves on edge and stirred an uneasy, restless mood in her.

She often thought about her husband's remark concerning every person's responsibility to defend society as well as himself and his family. He practiced exactly what he preached, she thought. It is certain that while a peaceful life is important, the responsibility of protecting this peace is incumbent upon everyone. Even if the Kugata family has fallen on hard times, the trouble will not have been in vain as long as it came about because they fulfilled their responsibility as human beings. I must believe in the rectitude of my husband's actions and protect my mother-in-law and Nobu without being distracted by nonessential things. Thoughts of this kind calmed her uneasiness.

She tried to avoid Teijiro as much as possible. Yet at times the effect of her thoughts was just the opposite, and she was very strongly tempted by Teijiro's way of life.

That man is not concerned with the public; he is not bound by the responsibility and duty of being a man. He thinks only about satisfying himself and living his life. He is afraid to die and is struggling to satisfy all his senses while he is alive. He says everyone must die and that good and evil, justice and injustice, truth and falsehood, one's failure or success in fulfilling one's obligations, all will have blown away like dust a thousand years from now. The one thing that's sure is that I am living right now. Isn't effort and suffering to satisfy oneself with supreme beauty and pleasure the true, human way to live?

Even during this period of spiritual unrest her work progressed. By the beginning of summer she had finished two pieces of flower matting with which she was reasonably satisfied. She was quite confident about one in particular. The border was an arabesque pattern, and in the center she had splashed orchid flowers and leaves, using thirteen different colors. She was still unable to correct discrepancies in the lines, and the mat was a bit too showy, but it was so beautiful that none of her productions could match it. One of the ill-natured housewives asked sarcastically whether she intended to make a formal kimono out of it. Old Mankichi was of course very happy for Ichi. It must have surpassed even Teijiro's expectations, for he mumbled, "It should be presented to the lord."

Ichi wanted to show it to her mother-in-law and obtained permission to bring the mat home.

"Oh, good! This is good!" Tatsuya peeped at it

over Iso's shoulder and shook his head as if deeply impressed. "Well, well, that's something. Really fantastic!"

"We can hardly tell whether you're praising it or not, Tatsuya." Iso burst into laughter. "Why is it so fantastic? It's very beautiful, isn't it?"

"Nobody would believe it's only a carpet. Don't misunderstand me—of course I'm praising it, sister. There's no reason not to praise it. It's great."

"But you sound as if you're belittling it." Laughing, Iso spread out the mat and picked up Nobu, who was lying beside it. "You should look at it too, Nobu. Your mother has made such a wonderful thing—a beautiful, wonderful flower mat which nobody ever made before. Your mother made that, Nobu. She's wonderful. Your mother is really wonderful."

Ichi felt warmly and directly that her mother-in-law was very happy for her. Iso had detested Ichi's going to work and had even seemed to be ashamed of it. Now perhaps she could be freed of her narrow ideas, since beauty makes everything good.

In any event, Ichi's work had been recognized and had impressed a few people. Nothing encourages a person and gives her greater power than this. Ichi passed that one night feeling cheerful, alive, and tense, and as if she wanted to thank everyone.

When she arrived at the weaving shop the following day, she was summoned to the main house for her first visit since her earlier conversation with Teijiro. She had been careful to avoid him, yet at the same time she had been tempted to do the opposite. Now, however, she was strangely free of unrest and suspicion and felt calm, with the strength of a person who had found her path.

Teijiro seemed to sense the difference in her attitude, and his treatment of her was visibly different. He praised her work on the flower mat and announced his intention to present it to Lord Toda. Then he told her that if she wanted any reference material for her work she would henceforth be allowed into this room at any time, that these objects were there for that purpose. He showed her many foreign books in the bookcase, beautiful fabrics, carpets with unusual and beautiful colors, and patterns stored in a cabinet.

"Since flower mats originated in the Western countries," he said, "I think it's a good idea to get some hints from these things."

Since his attitude was indicative of his hopes for this new work, Ichi was able to listen to him humbly, and she began to feel that she would happily accept his kind offer. Thinking that this was a good opportunity, she asked whether he would assign to her as an assistant the weaver Ume. Though Ume was only fifteen years old and did nothing but odd jobs, she was fond of Ichi, was witty, had a good memory, and was the kind of girl Ichi could depend on.

"I think it's all right." Teijiro did not raise any objection. "You may do whatever you like. But don't you think a girl that young is of no use to you? I think you should use another girl with slightly better skills."

"I think Ume's good for me after all. In many respects it's more important that she be young enough to do the job than that she be very skilled."

"Then why don't we hire more girls in that age category? Well, don't bother about my ideas—you'd better talk with Mankichi. Do whatever you think is best."

Ichi replied that she would work on it gradually and borrowed one of the reference books from the bookcase.

"It's all right now," she mumbled to herself on her way back to the weaving room. She had now put a distance between herself and Teijiro. Her work had begun. Teijiro could not move from his position, but she would make progress rapidly. The relationship between them was now definitely settled. Everything was going to be better.

It was a day of refreshing wind following the rainy season. Having decided to buy a toy for Nobu on her way home from the weaving shop, she went around to Karasue. At the corner of the street near the boat landing was a shop which sold odds and ends. Ichi went in and picked out a toy windmill with a wreath, a bisque creeping doll, and some needles and thread.

As she left the shop, she found a samurai lady dressed in traveling clothes waiting for her. "Ichi!" the lady called.

"Mother!" Ichi involuntarily cried out. She was about to run to the woman, when suddenly she became petrified.

"Mother!"

It was indeed her mother. Her eyes were wide open, her plump, round cheeks trembled, and her lips over the black-dyed teeth, the mark of the married woman, were open in a smile.

It's my mother. Oh, I must run away. But before this idea had occurred to Ichi, her mother was already approaching her with outstretched arms.

"Please don't run away, Ichi. I have something to tell you—something I must tell you—so please come with me, just over there."

"I . . . please let me go, mother."

"It won't take long. We'll finish quickly." Her mother was already holding Ichi's hand. "I shan't force you to come, but if you'll just listen to me, everything will be all right."

"Don't be frightened," said a voice behind her. She turned and saw Bennosuke, also in traveling clothes. "We'll let you go home soon."

Ichi felt herself turning pale. Bennosuke had been doing the same work as Shinzo but had been under suspicion by their colleagues. I thought he was my ally, and I don't know what kind of suspicions there were, but the mere fact that he's right here and safe must be proof of something. And if he's here, I can't possibly run away.

Ichi lowered her eyes and nodded. Her mother and Bennosuke, with Ichi between them, walked into a building which served as an agent's office, inn, and restaurant.

13

"THEN YOU had a baby." Her mother could hardly wait to sit down. She took the toy windmill and doll from Ichi's hand and looked at them, narrowing her eyes as if examining her grandchild. "It's already 300 days, I see . . . then she's crawling now. Do you have enough milk? . . . They say it's easier to raise a girl, but I guess the first one is really . . ."

While asking her all kinds of questions at once, the mother was studying her daughter's appearance: her hair style, her poor kimono and obi, her chapped fingers with their dye-stained tips. Ichi felt herself shrinking in fear from her mother's intense gaze, and she sat tensely with drooping head.

Her mother told her that she and Bennosuke had come to make a pilgrimage to the Ise Shrine. Then she mentioned that she intended to go down to Kuwana on a night boat, but could stay here tonight if it was not too inconvenient, for she was longing to talk with her daughter after such a long time, but what did Ichi think? Only then did she begin to talk about the Kugatas.

"I'm sure you know the things Shinzo did."

"I don't know," Ichi answered without raising her head. "He told me nothing. Besides, I thought it wasn't something a woman should stick her nose into."

"Then you don't even know about the punishment of the conspirators, do you?" The word "conspirators" had an ugly ring. "They were planning a revolution against the government. That's the greatest crime a samurai can commit, you know."

Ichi quietly raised her eyes and looked at Bennosuke, who was sitting nearby with arms crossed, looking at the river through the open *shoji* of the window. There was a look of dejection in his profile.

"I don't know anything about it." Ichi lowered her eyes again. "I don't know what my husband has done, or what kind of crime it is. But I do know what kind of personality he has and what kind of things he would be doing."

"You talk so naively, Ichi. If Shinzo is to be punished for committing a major crime, you have to be punished too. The result might stain the Okumura family name. Your father and I have been concerned about this. You don't know how hard we've been looking for you! Aside from this, consider your father's and my feelings and come back to us. We'll manage the situation somehow. You just come back to us, Ichi."

"But Nobu . . . my daughter's name is Nobu, mother, . . ." Ichi said, still looking down at her knees. "May I take Nobu with me?"

"I'm sure you can, since she's a girl. You are coming back to us, aren't you?"

"I'll go back to my house now, and then I'll return home with Nobu in four or five days."

"You are telling me the truth, aren't you? You're not cheating on me by saying nice things, are you, Ichi? Your father's been so worried his hair has gone completely white."

"Bennosuke can accompany me to my house," said Ichi, her eyes still downcast.

Ichi soon rose, saying that she would arouse suspicion if she got home too late. She gave the toy windmill and the doll to her mother, saying that it would be too much trouble for her to carry them herself, but what she meant was that she wanted her mother to have them as a substitute for holding Nobu in her arms.

Her mother seemed rather uneasy about Ichi's undue readiness to accept her offer and insisted that she wanted to talk more with her. But Ichi thought she would begin to scream if she listened to any more. Evading her mother's request as casually as she could, she said goodbye.

Bennosuke followed her out. It was already growing dark; a thick mist was flowing over the Makida River, and they could see snowy egrets soaring up from the reed bushes along the river bank. They went straight along the road, which turned toward Honmura in Shimada village, out to the river bank, and walked for a while.

Ichi stopped walking for a moment and looked at her brother. Bennosuke returned her gaze absent-mindedly, his face pale and expressionless. He had never been too healthy and had always had a gloomy face with scowling eyebrows. But now he seemed dejected and helpless, like a man in a stupor.

"Bennosuke, you knew what Shinzo was going to do, didn't you?" Ichi looked sharply into her brother's eyes. "You know very well that he wasn't going to commit a revolutionary crime, but rather to do exactly the opposite, brother."

"I don't know." Bennosuke's voice was dull and devoid of feeling, like water leaking from a cracked bowl. "I haven't the slightest idea what is just and unjust, or even whether there is such a thing as truth. Can you understand those things, Ichi?"

"What I want to know concerns him. I want to know what he and the people around him were planning and why they pleaded guilty to such a crime as revolution. I want to know how Shinzo died and what happened to Kyunosuke."

"Shinzo was run down in the castle, in the corridor leading from the accounting office to the bonfire room. But I know this only from other people, and I don't have any details."

"Then in that corridor . . . in that corridor he died?" Ichi's knees were trembling.

"Some say he was slain, some say he was captured, and I even heard that he escaped on the way to jail after his capture. We just don't know whether, or to what extent, the things people are saying about the events of that period are certain. Five people in addition to Gorobe Toda were slain, but I don't think Kyunosuke was among them. Eleven people from the public prosecutor's office were sent to prison. I think two of the *churo** were put under house arrest, and five were imprisoned in Edo. That's all I know."

"And they didn't accuse you of anything, Bennosuke?"

"*Me*? Why?" Bennosuke looked at his sister dully. "What do you mean by that?"

"I'm sure you did something called *Seishukufu*, brother. I remember conveying the message to you and that it was a great help to the work of Shinzo and his people."

"Nonsense!" Bennosuke smiled sardonically and waved his hand. "Such a thing has no meaning. I'm a buffoon. But I'm not the only one. Human beings are all buffoons. Those who do dishonest things and grow rich, those who make noises about justice and truth although they are powerless—in general they're all buffoons, and the strongest ones win. That's all there is to it. *Seishukufu!* Please, don't make me blush!"

Ichi stared at her brother's expressionless, mask-like face. He was like a man whose body and soul have been crushed and who is barely alive. He had been soft-hearted and sensitive, the closest brother to her in age and also the one whose personality was the most

* *Churo:* an official second in rank to the chief vassal.

compatible with hers, but he had changed completely. Like the master of Minojin House, but in a different way, this brother too had to be among the people left behind by the march of progress.

Ichi bowed to him, saying, "I'll say goodbye to you here," as if to encourage herself.

"Then you're not coming home, are you?"

"I want you to look after mother and father. They'll be angry at me. But since even you, Bennosuke, could escape without punishment, I don't think there's any need to worry that I'll ruin the family name. Take care of yourself."

Bennosuke answered her only with his eyes and looked after her without moving. She turned around after climbing down from the bank and walking a hundred yards along the footpath between the rice fields. Bennosuke, still gazing after her, was silhouetted against the gloomy, dim light of dusk.

My husband may still be alive. It was a most precious and, for Ichi, an incomparable piece of news. There seemed to be no proof that he was alive, but there also seemed to be no definite proof that he was dead. Since she had almost completely given up hope for his life, it was almost unbearable to return to a state of uncertainty, but she was nevertheless happy to have the hope of that one chance in a million.

At the same time she could hardly bear the thought that they had pleaded guilty to "planning a revolution." Of course she could not understand the details, since it had something to do with politics, but she simply could not believe that the conviction for planning a revolution was just. Probably the opposition had manipulated the matter through the power they wielded in order to protect their own existence. Bennosuke had also said that the strongest man would win, which showed that in the present circumstances the strongest man had won, without regard for the right and wrong of the actual facts.

Such a thing shouldn't be permitted. Ichi shook her head as she walked quickly along the darkening path toward her house. It can't just end like this! No! If my husband's work, for which he sacrificed his own family and his own life as well, is the proper course to take in order to fulfill one's responsibility as a human being, I should not watch in silence while it is squelched as a "revolution." Whatever I have to do, whatever hardships I have to face, I must.

Upon her return to the house she asked Josuke to step outside, and consulted him about moving. She gave as a pretext the fact that since she had met Bennosuke at Karasue a search for them must be going on in the area. She made no mention of the fact that her mother had been there, nor did she say anything about her husband and Kyunosuke.

Her mother-in-law and even Tatsuya became tense when they heard the news, and Josuke too was at a loss.

"If that's the way things are," said the old man, "I guess you should move somewhere else for a while, for instance to the territory of the Takasu clan." He began to think. "I have someone in mind, just outside Morishima. He used to be a farm hand here at my place, and now he's farming a little place of his own. This man would make no complaints, even if we went to him right now. But . . . well, his house is a very dirty place. . . ."

"Since this is such an emergency, we'll be all right as long as we can just take shelter somewhere. Right, mother?"

"You're right, but . . ." Iso closed her eyes for a moment. "But I'm afraid we're only asking him for our own convenience. And since we've given so much trouble already . . ."

"Don't talk like that. And if you can put up with the inconvenience, Tatsuya and I can even carry your things there tonight," said Josuke.

"I'd be very happy if you could," Ichi said, paying no attention to her mother-in-law. "We'll think about the next steps later. We'd like to leave here as soon as possible."

"Good. . . . It's all very . . . it was all a very nice dream," said Tatsuya, his body swaying as if in a trance. "I thought we could settle down here. If things go on like this, I guess my field won't amount to anything."

Ichi stood up and went to pack.

14

"SINCE Ogasa is near the border of the Takasu clan territory, it's a convenient refuge in case of emergency."

Tatsuya's words were now proving true. The family transported their belongings there that very night, and the following morning, before daybreak, Ichi tied Nobu to her back, took her mother-in-law's hand, and left Josuke's house. If they went to another clan's territory, there was not the slightest possibility that their whereabouts would be discovered, so long as they did not become official residents there.

Ichi's worry had not been without foundation. Thorough searches were carried out all over Sakamatsu Prefecture for more than ten days and Josuke and his wife were questioned on numerous occasions, but ultimately no trace of Ichi, Iso, and Tatsuya was found.

Since the rainy season had gone without a hitch this year and the sunshine was also perfect, people were saying that the crop would surely be a good one. All the villages were happily discussing plans for the summer festival entertainment.

Morishima was near the Nagara River. It was commonly called Senmachida, or One Thousand Fields, and the name was apt. Everywhere were lowlands planted with rice and lotus. A ridge with a row of pine trees cut through the approximate center of the village as far as the river; this was called the Karesawa, or Dry Marsh, and was a kind of dike built to protect against flooding.

Mozaemon's house, where Ichi and her family had taken refuge, stood near the southern side of this dike. The house and storage building were built on a stone foundation five feet high. Mozaemon, his wife, Toshi, and their one child tilled a rice field of about two and a half acres and raised carp in the lotus pond.

Both husband and wife were completely unsociable people. They were simple and stupidly honest rather than upright, and their only pleasure was earning money. Their five-year-old child, known as Hei (his real name was not used), bore an almost uncanny resemblance to his parents in features and personality. He puttered about quietly and played all by himself, either in the field or in the house. His activities consisted of imitating his parents' farm work or whittling a piece of wood into a small hoe or a plow. It was amusing to watch him assume a very serious air, as if he were earning a living like a full-fledged adult.

A seven-year-old child named Kiichi lived nearby. Hei was quite a solitary child with no particularly close friend, but whenever he saw Kiichi he was sure to go out and call him all kinds of bad names.

"Kiichi's got a bald spot on his head," Hei would shout. "If a fly lands there, it'll slide right off!"

Then Kiichi would rush over, thrust his head in front of Hei, and say, "Take a good look at me. Do I got a bald patch on my head? See, I ain't got none!"

Hei would look closely at his head, then nod, saying, "No, you don't got none."

"I don't got no bald patch," Kiichi would say with his small shoulders squared. "The bald patch is on *your* head. Unnerstan'?"

"Yeah."

"You're the baldyhead," Kiichi would emphasize, and go away. Then Hei would again shout the nasty remark after him. "Kiichi's got a bald spot on his head. If a fly lands there . . ."

Then Kiichi would come running back, hit Hei on the head, and quickly run off.

Ichi watched this scene from her borrowed room in the storage building, and it made her laugh. When she noticed that even her mother-in-law was watching them laughingly, she would think about how it would be if Nobu were a boy and would somehow feel sorry that her child had been born a girl. Then she would take the sleeping baby in her arms and press her to her breast.

Early in July Ichi went to Shimada. She had not gone to Minojin House since the recent events, and she wanted to make her excuses and tell them that she was in hiding. She had gone to the trouble of choosing a rainy day because she could disguise her appearance a little with rain gear. She left the house, looking like a man in her straw sandals, straw coat, and straw hat.

The distance to Minojin House now was twice what it had been from Ogasa, and since the wind had begun blowing from south to north and the rain become stronger, the trip took Ichi even longer than she had expected. When she finally reached Minojin House even her undergarments were soaking wet under the straw coat. However, she did not stop at the weaving shop, but visited the main house just as she was.

"Well, well, to come in such a rain!" Mankichi came out as if meeting someone he longed to see and helped her out of the hat and coat. "I heard the story in Ogasa and figured you wouldn't come around here for a while. But since we've received a very pleasant order from the castle. . . . Oh dear! You're soaked!"

"No, not really. I'm just going to tell Teijiro that I can't come any more, and then I'll head for home."

"If you stay in those wet clothes, you'll catch cold. I'll order some dry clothes for you to change into, so take those wet ones off and I'll hang them to dry. They'll dry in no time in the drying room. . . ."

The old man went into the back room. A middle-aged female servant soon came in with a change of clothes and an obi for Ichi. While she was in the bathroom drying her wet body and changing her kimono, Ichi realized that the weather had become extremely violent; the wind was blowing so hard it was ripping at the eaves, and the pouring rain was slapping objects around and making a screen of water.

Typical of people brought up in this area, she would soon begin to worry about flooding if this weather continued. "I hope it won't flood," she mumbled, and for a while she uneasily watched the driving rain.

Mankichi then led her to Teijiro's room. The master, his face swollen as if from a sleepless night, was just opening a book on the desk, but when he saw Ichi he placed a piece of paper over the book to hide it, and, pressing the paper with his long pale fingers, greeted her.

"That mat has become famous." Teijiro began to talk as soon as Ichi had sat down. "I'm sure I told you that we were going to present it to Lord Toda, and soon after I last saw you we did just that. About five days ago he summoned us to him, so I sent Mankichi, who reported back to me that the lord was very pleased and had asked him for details about the maker of the mat."

"I hope Mankichi didn't tell him about me!"

"Of course he didn't tell him about your social position. He said he told the lord only that it had been made by a lady who was supporting her elderly mother and her small child and that she had designed it herself without instruction from anyone. We were again summoned the day before yesterday and ordered to bring you to the castle. You're to have the honor of an audience with the lord."

For a moment Ichi's breath stopped. It was a very rare honor for an ordinary subject of no social standing to be granted the honor of an audience with the lord;

it was absolutely unthinkable to refuse. If Ichi declined, not even Minojin House could escape punishment for the crime of disrespect.

"What shall I do!" Ichi involuntarily raised imploring eyes. "If I go to Ogaki they'll soon find out who I am. I simply cannot accept the summons."

"I thought about that too. As you well know, this is something we simply cannot refuse. Furthermore, since this will be of tremendous advantage to our work in the future, I'd like you to accept this summons regardless of the cost. The thing is to change your appearance. What do you think?"

"You say change my appearance, but . . ."

"Oh, you'll change it completely. It's a pity, but you'll color your cheeks up to your hair and make a scar or burn mark on your face. You'll also change your hairdo and your kimono and obi. I think you'll be all right then."

Ichi shuddered, but thought that if she were made up that heavily her identity could be successfully concealed. Teijiro then told her that Minojin House would probably win an award for the mat and that they would certainly receive good news at that time about, for instance, the subsidy for the manufacture of the new flower mats and permission to replant the bingo-rush, both of which they had already requested.

Meanwhile the wind was blowing more and more violently, and the driving rain was shooting silver arrows in every direction from a terrifyingly dark sky. Since Ichi was feeling increasingly uneasy, she answered that she would return in a few days after she had thought the matter over thoroughly. Then she stood up to leave.

The master looked out through the window and then said a strange thing.

"I think I must have the nature of a beast," he said. "When the weather turns so stormy, I become strangely high-spirited. Usually I feel bored and tired, but when I look at wind and rain I become incredibly cheerful. I feel like running stark naked up the mountain or jumping and rolling around carefree in a bamboo grass field, or in the woods, or in the rocky gorge. . . . I guess it's indecent to say this in front of you, but . . . a beautiful woman . . . a beautiful young woman with a healthy, well-proportioned body . . . stripping her, running around wildly in the mountains where the violent wind and driving rain are roaring madly, running her down, her escaping, grabbing and grappling with her and rolling down the stony slope . . . oh! I can see it! I can feel it!"

Shouting, Teijiro turned around abruptly to face her. He stared at Ichi with bloodshot, glaring eyes, and took one large step forward. But at that very moment he covered his face with his hands and groaned, "Please go away. Quick, go away! Please go away!"

Ichi rushed out of the room like a madwoman.

She got ready, still wearing the borrowed kimono, and left Minojin House. The worried Mankichi asked her to wait for a while and see whether the storm would pass, or at least to have lunch. Since he was so visibly worried about flooding, Ichi herself grew nervous, and she left without saying goodbye.

Since the wind was against her, she was soaked to the skin after walking only two or three hundred feet. The rice paddy around her was full of waves like a turbulent sea, and many of the young trees along the road had been blown down. Her straw coat and hat were constantly being ripped off, and torn branches and leaves flying through the air hit her cheeks, hands, and legs.

While she was thinking about how her mother-in-law must be worrying, and whether Nobu was frightened, the recollection of Teijiro's large, bloodshot eyes, his strange words, and his frightening attitude went through her mind. She could not rid herself of the dread that she was being pursued. She could not forget his proud manner when he said that he must have the nature of a beast, and she could also picture his vision of rolling about naked on the mountain in a stormy, driving rain as vividly as if she were seeing it with her own eyes.

Not only are his nerves shot—he really does have an eccentric personality. He makes much of satisfying the senses above all else, but perhaps the person who is dominated by the senses may be the person closest to the beast.

When she reached Otagiri along the way, she found men in straw coats and hats running about with poles and *mokko,* the woven straw carts used to carry mud and sand.

"Did they open the dam?" "We've got to destroy it!" She heard shouted snatches of such conversation, and there was wild excitement among the people putting mud into straw bags and carrying them to the assigned places.

Frightened, Ichi began to run for her life against the rain and wind slapping against her.

* * *

Part Four

15

 FEW DETAILS of her experience that night remained in Ichi's memory. It was like the memory of her departure from the house in Ogaki; she was uncertain which event occurred first, and her impression of the experience was fragmentary.

When she reached the house, Tatsuya was not there; being worried about her, he had left about an hour earlier to look for her. Mozaemon and his wife were moving items of furniture which could not easily be transported to the second story of the storage building and were taking clothes and bedding by wagon to Takahata.

"I think everything will probably turn out all right, but we've never had such stormy weather," Mozaemon stuttered. "If you have anything important, please give it to me, I'll transport everything in one trip. If you're not taking anything you can escape along the Karesawa. Well, I guess everything will turn out all right."

As is always the case with people in an area alert to flood danger, he acted cautiously but was not very frightened.

At Iso's insistence, Ichi got their things together and asked Mozaemon to carry out the very large items. For a moment she had a dim recollection of a very important object which she had to take with her whenever she fled in emergencies. What was it? "However you do it . . . but in absolute safety . . ." The words rang vaguely in her mind, but she could not recollect what the object was.

While she and Iso were packing, Mozaemon's wife came in and asked about getting milk for Nobu. Since their arrival here they had been getting milk for her in the neighborhood. Since Nobu would soon have her first birthday, Ichi was gradually weaning her to solid food, but the baby did better if she could get milk twice a day.

"We should feed her well now, and I'll ask the wet nurse to squeeze out a little milk as a precaution," said Toshi, and she went out with Nobu in her arms.

When the packing was finished, Mozaemon piled their belongings on the wagon and left, with Hei pushing. The room, made untidy by a lunch box containing rice balls and by the bundles into which they had put their personal belongings, was so dark they longed for a light.

"Since our departure from Ogaki we've done nothing but pack and run," Iso said laughingly. "Hundreds of years ago when the Heishi family was made to run from Kyoto, they must have felt the same way, but I'm already getting a bit bored."

Ichi did not know what answer to make and took advantage of the fact that the water was boiling to say that she would go and make tea.

The broken oiled-paper *shoji* in the kitchen was rattling in the wind, with a noise like the buzzing of insects. By comparison with the roar of the violent storm it sounded so peaceful, like the hum of a bee.

Just as she was thinking that the *shoji* sounded like a flute, Ichi remembered the small parcel which her husband had asked her to keep safe and which she had brought with her from Ogaki.

Where did I put it? Ichi jumped up. Where is it?

Almost everything had been carried out. It definitely was not among the bundles left behind. Where was it! She tried quickly to remember, but her efforts only confused her brain and made her dizzy.

I don't remember it! . . . If it's definitely here, it can only be in that bundle. There were the expensive things I brought with me from home when I got married. I kept them stored away in the humble Kugata house, but took them with me when we left Ogaki, thinking they might be useful. There was one extra bundle I took with me then. I've been so busy since my arrival in Ogasa, giving birth to a child and doing other things . . . did I forget it and put it into that bundle?

She had a faint recollection of doing just that.

Then I've got to get it back quickly. Something my

husband so insistently begged me to care for shouldn't go out of my hands.

Ichi quickly ran downstairs and rushed outside, pulling on the straw coat and hat. She heard her mother-in-law calling "Ichi!" but she simply shouted back that she would return soon and ran down the stone steps. Since Tatsuya would surely be back soon she felt she could leave her mother-in-law in his care. She also believed that although she knew only the general direction to Takahata she would be able to reach the men before they had traveled too far, since there was only one road and the men were dragging the wagon.

It was no easy matter, however, to travel the unfamiliar road in the darkness and rain. She accidentally took the wrong turn and made a number of mistakes, and since there was no one around to assist her she lost a great deal of time. Finally she found the wagon just at the entrance to Takahata village.

How impatient she was, when they had said that the village was only a step further, to force the wagon to stop and to search for the object she had in mind! How happy she was to finally find that particular bundle and that particular parcel in the bundle! It was like a dream.

Ichi immediately turned back toward home. Mozaemon shouted, "Let's go to Takahata together. They say the dam has broken at Tomieki." Paying no heed, Ichi fastened the parcel to her back and went back down the road.

I've found the parcel my husband asked me to care for! I have it with me now! Nothing satisfied her more than this feeling. It brought back to her mind all the things she had forgotten. . . . I woke up at midnight and couldn't get back to sleep, and went into my husband's bedroom, unable to suppress my longing. . . . I found out then for the first time, with such an overwhelming physical pleasure, that Shinzo was really my husband. . . . That night when he spoke to me about this parcel, how soothed and sweet I felt when my husband came to me under my mosquito netting, wiped off my perspiration with a cold, wet towel, and fanned me. . . .

Her most trivial feelings and delicate sensations on these occasions flashed through her mind as vividly as if she were experiencing them at that very moment. It was such a clear and immediate sensation that it almost aroused involuntary convulsions in her body.

I loved my husband, and he loved me. . . . He answered my insistent questions that time by saying that my idea that husband and wife are two acting as one was not true and that a human being is always alone no matter how long he lives. I thought this a very cold idea, but it was simply that the sureness and depth of my husband's love were stronger than the vague idea that husband and wife act only as one. His saying entirely honestly that a human being is always alone no matter how long he lives is proof that my husband loved me as a human being. He really loved me!

Ichi hurried along, half running and driven by an intoxicated joy, stopping every now and then to check that the parcel was still on her back. When she came to the turn she found it flooded knee-high. The wind was as strong as ever, the rain was heavy, and it was already dark. Ichi felt that if she hesitated she would miss her way, so she went right into the water.

She was never able to describe the confusion which followed. She fell into the deep water up to her hips and was almost swept away. She frequently asked questions of people making their escape in the streets. She thought that the moon was peeping out once in a while from between the clouds, which were running at frightening speed, and yet the rain was still slapping her cheeks. She would never forget the heartbreaking voices of children calling their parents, the distraught voices of mothers looking for their children. She was told that there was no hope left for Morishima, and she made sure that everybody had escaped to Karesawa. She later found out that the dike of the Nagara River had broken faster than even the old men who were natives of this area had expected, and people said that a tremendous amount of dirty water had engulfed the villages downriver from Otagiri.

When Ichi finally reached Karesawa, it was crowded with people and their belongings piled up on the dike. Even here she heard voices in the violent wind, shouting out sharply or sadly for parents, children, husbands, wives. Ichi added her voice to the tumult, shouting "Mother!" as she ran about in the crowd.

Finally she heard her mother-in-law answer her, and with a feeling of indescribable excitement Ichi found her sitting under a big pine tree. Iso had placed a straw hat on her head and was seated with Nobu in her arms, not far from their bundles of personal belongings. Mozaemon's wife and two or three wives from her neighborhood were also there.

"What happened to you?" Iso asked in an unexpectedly calm, quiet voice. She put the straw mat over Ichi. "It doesn't matter about me, but did you have to leave Nobu behind?"

"Shinzo asked me to keep something for him." Ichi quickly took Nobu into her own arms. "It was something very important which I should have kept with me, but I carelessly put it into a bundle which went in the wagon. So I went after it, thinking that Tatsuya would soon be back and that it wouldn't take me long to find the wagon and then get back to the house."

"I don't think Tatsuya's back yet. He's such an easygoing person," Iso said. Her voice revealed her pleasure at being together with her daughter-in-law. "He might have gone to Shimada and then been unable to get back. He's probably saying it's rather a big flood."

She sounded exactly like Tatsuya. Ichi burst into laughter. Then she put her straw coat on Nobu and held the baby tightly. Turning to Mozaemon's wife, she told her that she had seen Mozaemon and Hei at Takahata and that the two would probably stay there.

She was just about to open a lunch box for her mother-in-law when a strange shout and a stir came from the upper part of the dike, and she felt the ground sway. Until now the crowd around them had seemed to be settled down for the time being; people had talked to each other in loud voices and even laughed once in a while. But now all voices and movements stopped, and the sound of the roaring storm bent over the crowd and covered it with its horrifying clarity and determined pressure. Nothing overwhelmed the people more than this momentary silence.

When the ground swayed, Ichi squeezed Nobu in her arms. The pressure must have been too strong, for Nobu began to cry. But the fear, horror, and despair were so overriding that Ichi could not think to loosen her arms even as she listened to the baby cry.

THE KARESAWA dike, a place of refuge in floods, ran through Takahata as far as Tsurana. The flood had poured over from Otagiri to the west, attacked the dike below Takahata, and broken it down about a half mile up-river from where Ichi and her family were sitting.

Once broken, the dike crashed down from end to end, and the crowd of people who had taken refuge on it, and their belongings, were carried away by the water.

Ichi discovered what was happening from the shouts of the people who were rushing toward this spot like a landslide. Half unconsciously she undid the hemp rope around the bundles and tied one end around her mother-in-law, the other end around herself.

"Don't bother about me, take care of Nobu," Iso seemed to be saying.

Ichi had put the crying Nobu on the ground. She could not see the baby in the darkness; the sight of Nobu kicking off the straw coat and crying loudly would remain in her memory with painful vividness.

She could never remember later whether she fastened the rope around the pine, or whether it clung to the tree accidentally. It was not true that she weighed her mother-in-law and Nobu in the balance and decided to help her mother-in-law by abandoning Nobu. Yet it was true that she screamed, "Forgive me, Nobu! Forgive me, Nobu!" and that she constantly put her hand to the parcel on her back to make sure it was there.

"You must help Nobu!" Iso seemed to be repeating. But when the ground fell and another pitch black ground surged up in its place, Ichi held her mother-in-law in her arms and clung to the pine tree.

The rest was an incoherent nightmare. She was swallowed up in the water, someone's hand coiled fast around her neck, choking her. Something knocked

her violently in the stomach, and her hair was pulled
so hard it seemed it would be torn off. She felt her
whole body being turned in circles, and many hands
slapped her face.

In this dark, chaotic world, before she lost consciousness, Ichi heard a voice singing very vividly,

> If the mountain burns down,
> The mother bird will run away.
> There is nothing more precious
> Than her own life.

It was Nobu's voice.

Ichi and her mother-in-law were narrowly saved
when, still clinging to the pine tree by means of the
rope, they were swept into the bushes in the village
of Kajita. They regained consciousness three or four
days later, thanks to the care of the villagers. They
looked at each other, felt each other, and realized that
they were still alive.

Her mother-in-law stretched out her hand, stroked
Ichi's hair, and wet her pillow with endless tears.
Though she said not a word, Ichi understood what
Iso's tears were saying. She herself did not cry, but
took her mother-in-law's hand and stroked it, nodding
to her quietly.

I understand, mother. It must be true. Since Nobu
has already become a little Buddha, I am sure she must
be pleased about these things, she thought, stroking
Iso's hand sympathetically. Strangely enough, she did

not feel sad. But what she could hardly bear was the
fact that when she dozed off she could hear that voice
singing the cruel, hurtful phrase that the mother bird
would run away when in danger, those scornful words
that she would try to save herself even if she had to
abandon her baby bird because there was nothing more
precious than her own life. The fact that the voice was
obviously Nobu's was unbearable. It couldn't be possible—the two sets of circumstances were completely
different. That song had been sung by the ill-natured
housewife at Minojin House; it was absolutely impossible that Nobu would think such a thing. It must
all be a delusion. But immediately after reasoning
along this line, she would again hear the song.

The first thing Ichi did after she was able to get out
of bed was to spread out and dry the contents of the
parcel she had carried on her back. It contained five
bound volumes, and each volume had a title. At first
she tried to be cautious, so that the books would not
be seen, but as they dried she began to read the titles,
and then, giving in to temptation, their contents.

There were five books of records, entitled "Events
that Should be Criticized and Corrected," "Financial
Summary," "The Party Cliques," "Conspiracy Surrounding the Adoption of a Child as a Successor to the
Ruler," and *Seishukufu* (List of Constellations). They
contained an exact record of more than ten years of
injustice and corruption among the major vassals surrounding Otaka, the chief vassal of the territory.

What surprised Ichi most was the fact that her

father's name clearly appeared in "The Party Cliques" and in "Conspiracy Surrounding the Adoption of a Child." The *Seishukufu* was written in Bennosuke's familiar hand, and therefore she did not find their father's name in it. But the name of Kasho Okumura appeared in every other document. In particular, he was named as one of the chief conspirators in the effort to circumvent the will of Lord Toda concerning the adoption of his successor.

It all shocked Ichi beyond belief. Far more surprising, however, was her keen awareness of the effort put into this report and the miserable fruits of that effort. These five books were filled with the bleeding cries of people who had committed the crime of "revolution," people who had been slain on the streets, run down in the castle like her husband, felt the sword on their *hakama* like Kyunosuke, and seen themselves and their families thrown into prison.

Not everything written was necessarily the truth; the truth was really in the hearts of those who had carried out the investigation. It had proved impossible to sully the purity of heart of those who had worked for proper reform of the clan government and for the happiness of the clan's law-abiding citizens, and this only proved that their action was the exact opposite of a "revolution."

Ichi felt she should show these documents to everyone and petition for establishment of the truth about this matter. Then she realized that she might have an opportunity to see the lord himself, for the flower mat which Minojin House had presented to him was her entree to the honor of an audience. If she were lucky, she might be able to petition Lord Toda then.

Ichi began to tremble.

No, it's not a question of whether I can or can't—I *must* do it. I don't know what kind of formalities will be required to obtain an audience, but as long as I can go before him, nothing is impossible if I give up my own life. There must be one thing which will attract his attention. As long as I have this plan . . .

Stories about the calamity were spreading far and wide; more than ten houses had been swept away in one place, many people had died, a whole village had been completely wiped out, hundreds of dead bodies were found at this or that dike, so many fields were under water, so many completely destroyed, and so on. Normally rumors of this type would have died away naturally, but this time they increased, giving numbers of houses, people, domestic animals, and fields, and it was even rumored that famine throughout the Mino region could no longer be avoided.

Completely unconcerned, Ichi turned a deaf ear to the rumors. Her mind was filled with one thing alone. The bright, clear, completely windless days continued, and the mud-covered fields stretched for endless miles under the dazzling sun. The now cloudy water formed an enormous lake. Branches thrust their heads up from the water, and villages became visible, their rooftops forming islands. But even these scenes seemed remote and uninteresting to Ichi. She looked at them

with her eyes, but her mind was concerned with
something else.

There were about thirty refugees in the straw hut
where Ichi and her mother-in-law were receiving
assistance. This village alone, it was said, had five such
huts. The sorrow and despair of these people who had
lost their fields, belongings, parents, children, and
husbands and wives did not move Ichi.

Moans and sobs were heard in the night, Iso's among
them. She would cry out, "Nobu! Nobu!" and sob
for a long time. She had lost her first grandchild.
Worse yet, that child had been abandoned before her
very eyes, and in her stead. If she had not lived, the
baby might have been saved. Iso was unable to banish
this idea from her mind, and the sound of her voice
calling her grandchild was enough to break any lis-
tener's heart. Ichi could understand Iso's feelings, but
she herself was completely numb and unable to shed
even a single tear, and her mind was cheerless and
calm.

When I come before Lord Toda, she would
think, gazing at the pitch black night sky and listening
to her mother-in-law's sobs, how can I attract his
attention? How? . . .

On the seventh morning after the flood Ichi went
out to Takahata. The distance was under two miles, but
the road was flooded, and here and there it was barred
by mud, trees, or ruined houses washed down from
farther up the river. She was forced into so many
detours that the trip took her a long time. Takahata

was not flooded, and it presented an incredibly peaceful scene, except for the emergency aid hut.

After four or five inquiries she found Mozaemon and his son in the garden of a house. Hei was watching an ant lion under the persimmon tree, and Mozaemon, his hands absent-mindedly stuck into his belt, was watching a dragonfly flitting about. When Ichi called him, he grinned emptily. In a moment, however, the grinning face turned pale and stiffened.

"My wife is . . ." he murmured. "How is Toshi?"

Ichi turned around silently. Hei was standing under the persimmon tree and looking in her direction with his big, earnest, almost pleading eyes.

Ichi looked straight into Mozaemon's eyes and told him, "I want you to get my belongings." Then, without looking at his face she went over to the persimmon tree, bent down, and took Hei in her arms. The child tried to push her away. Ichi held him across her bent knees and pressed her cheeks softly against his hard, sunburnt ones. She wanted to say that his mother would be back soon, but her tongue would not move and no sound came out. The child indicated his dislike and, slipping out of Ichi's arms, ran away.

"Since Morishima is still under water, we can't go back," Mozaemon said absent-mindedly. "My horses have gone, and it seems that the storage building was smashed . . . the water came too quickly. . . . There are worse places. The mountain fell in Harui. . . ."

Ichi took out one parcel from her bundles, tied them up again, and asked him to keep them in his charge for a while longer. Mozaemon accompanied her to the road. His stupidly honest face was still white and stiff, and he frequently raised his bony black hand and rubbed the back of his neck.

"Well, then . . . so you are staying in Kajita," he murmured, looking at the ground, when they were about to separate. "Please tell the old lady that I'm keeping her belongings in my charge for their safety. And that the child and I are safe. Please tell her that."

As she turned onto the road, a voice called from behind her, "Auntie!" Turning around, she saw Hei peeping at her through the screen of bushes.

"Auntie!" he called again. Ichi nodded to him and paused as if to say something, but then she turned onto the road and began walking.

17

 ON HER way back to Kajita she heard a rumor, apparently well substantiated, that Lord Toda was inspecting the flood district. He was said to have shown up at one village the other day and to have spent the night in yet another. She also heard detailed stories from a person who had actually seen his retinue.

He must be coming to Shimada village, too, Ichi thought, and decided that if so this would be her best opportunity. An audience with him merely for the sake of a flower mat might be postponed by others after such a great calamity, but it provided Ichi an excuse to try to have an audience quickly. Ichi almost ran the rest of the way to Kajita.

"Oh! What about Tatsuya?" Iso said the moment she saw Ichi. "Isn't Tatsuya with you?"

"Is Tatsuya safe?"

"But you . . ." Then her mother-in-law stopped breathing for a second and smiled a twisted smile. "How foolish I am . . . I'm sorry. I guess I dozed off and was dreaming. Sorry to have said such a foolish thing to you. I thought you were talking with Tatsuya as you came along the road. I even heard it so clearly."

"I want to leave for Shimada right now." Ichi deliberately paid no attention to her mother-in-law. "I have an idea. I'm afraid it may be two days before I'm able to return. . . . I want to stop in Ogasa to see Josuke."

"I'm all right now; I could go too—but do you think the roads are still bad?"

"I think that for a while longer it will still be hard for you to get around, since it's still flooded and the roads have been destroyed. . . . I'll return as soon as possible."

Ichi spoke in a blunt, unusually determined manner which Iso had never seen before, so she said nothing more and merely watched her daughter-in-law uneasily. Ichi left the hut without waiting for the free rice-soup lunch.

The parcel she had brought back to Kajita contained valuable hair pieces, combs, and mirrors which she had brought in her trousseau. She had brought them out now with the intention of selling them.

An autumn wind was blowing, but the midday sunshine was hot enough to burn her skin; since the red mud which had come down from the mountain had dried and now whirled dustily whenever the wind blew, her eyes, mouth, ears, and even the roots of her hair were immediately covered with dust. Everywhere a free rice-soup lunch was being served in huts crowded with half-naked men, women, and children. People were saying that an epidemic was spreading, and posters forbidding the drinking of unboiled water were displayed everywhere. Even the dried areas and the rice paddies, not to mention the fields which had been destroyed or were under water, were covered with a whitish mud. The plants swaying in the wind made an empty noise like the sound produced by rubbing sawdust.

Ichi looked at these sights without the slightest emotion. She did not knit her eyebrows or change color at the vision of even the most painful scene, but merely hurried on her way northward, looking straight ahead coldly and without expression.

It was about eight o'clock in the evening when she finally reached Minojin House. She had heard that this area too had been attacked by the water. The weaving shop was stripped and bore not the slightest resemblance to its previous appearance, and more than half of the willow trees that had served as a fence had fallen down. But the main house had been saved; only the *tatami* downstairs had gotten wet.

Old Mankichi, dressed only in his undergarments, was puttering about, but when he saw Ichi coming he shouted in surprise and rushed to meet her, throwing down what he was holding. Ichi went forward to greet him, but suddenly everything turned black before her eyes, and she fell, stretching out her arms in search of something to clutch for support. The ground of the cold unfloored area felt pleasantly fresh and cool. Then she felt as if she were sinking, and she lost consciousness, overcome by hunger, fatigue, and heat.

She regained consciousness around midnight and found that she was lying under a large 20-mat mosquito netting while Mankichi was moving the fan at the head of the bed.

Ichi made sure that the parcel was beside her. Then she quietly turned her head and asked him, "Have we had a visit from the lord yet?"

The old man looked at her with a puzzled expression, apparently believing that she was in a delirium.

Ichi moistened her sticky tongue and asked again, more clearly, "Have you had a visit yet from Lord Toda?"

"Not yet, my lady," the old man answered soothingly, making a breeze with the fan. "He was supposed to visit us today, but it was postponed for reasons connected with the schedule of his retinue."

"Oh, I see . . . good, good."

"I'm lucky; that was a narrow escape," she murmured to herself, and fell back to sleep as if drugged into slumber.

By morning her fever had not abated and when she got up her head swam, so that she could not walk without being supported by a servant. She had no appetite and suffered from severe headache and nausea. But she was straining every nerve, and when Teijiro paid her a visit she immediately told him, "I should like to have an audience if the lord comes."

Teijiro started to say something, but Ichi interrupted him. "It's the only request I'll ever make in my life," she pleaded several times. "I shan't make any trouble for you."

The fact was that Minojin House had been designated a rest house for Lord Toda, and preparations to receive him had already been made downstairs. Since Ichi had already received a summons for an audience, it would not be difficult for her to see him as long as she was not sick. It was her health that made Teijiro hesitate. He was thinking that the officers would soon be arriving, that if they found out there was a sick person in the house he would be punished, and that he must move her somewhere now. But he realized that the manner in which Ichi expressed her request was not normal. The eager expression in her eyes, which were dimmed with fever, had a desperate power which would not allow him to refuse her. Turning to Mankichi he said, "You'd better move her to the storeroom, even if it is hot there." Then, standing up to leave, he told Ichi to be ready to move.

"I think Lord Toda will visit this afternoon, so you'd better be well rested by then. You can't do anything unless you're able to get out of bed. I'll manage the rest somehow."

"I'm all right. I'll definitely get up." Ichi twisted her face violently. She was attacked by a wave of severe dizziness and nausea, and just as she was deciding to fight it off she fainted again.

The intervening events before her appearance seemed to be without any order, as if one were looking piecemeal at a picture scroll. But when the appointed time approached she got up, sent the maid for cosmetics, and fixed her hair and made up her face with the maid's help. The cosmetics had belonged to Teijiro's wife, who had returned to her parents' home, and they were old and dried out, but at least they served to hide her sickly pallor. She cut an irregular patch out of a piece of brown silk fabric for a disguise and pasted it on her right cheek. Then she lay down again, listened to people's steps and the noise of the officers who seemed to have just arrived, and fell back into her uneasy, paralyzing half-sleep.

When Teijiro came in with Mankichi, Ichi immediately opened her eyes. She sat up with the same naturalness with which she had just come out of her sleep.

"You shouldn't try too hard." Teijiro came close to

her. He was wearing *kamishimo,* or formal dress, and the white socks known as *tabi.* "Don't force yourself too hard until you come before Lord Toda. Since I told them only that you were not feeling too well, everything will be all right."

"I can get up." Ichi lightly held the parcel, which she had put in her kimono sleeve, and stood up like a different person. "I can walk all by myself. Are there many attendants around?"

"Only four, plus one major vassal."

"What's his name?"

"Chikara Toda, they say."

A very faint smile curved Ichi's lips. What would I do if it were my father? had been her only fear. If she had heard Teijiro say Kasho Okumura, Ichi would have been paralyzed.

She followed quietly after Teijiro.

A special exception had evidently been made, because of her indisposition, for her to be received on the veranda instead of in the garden. Lord Toda was seated in the highest seat, surrounded by a curtain bearing his family crest. To his left and right sat four or five samurai.

When Teijiro had finished his introduction, a voice asked the two to raise their heads. The lord, dressed in a linen kimono and *hakama,* proved to be a man with a long, dark, tired face. On his hip was a very ordinary small sword in a black-lacquered sheath. Every so often he coughed dryly and rather severely, wiping his lips with tissue paper. He praised Ichi for the magnificence of the flower mat she had recently made and, after thanking her for her service, inquired about the design of her machine.

"Please allow me to answer Your Highness directly," Ichi said. Then, her face still bowed, she answered his questions. She felt perfectly calm and was able to speak clearly. She explained to him as simply as she could how she had felt when she saw the flower mat for the first time, about the things that had happened since she had been hired by Minojin House, and about the sincere help of the master and his servants, which perhaps had been more decisive than her own efforts. She told him that she thought she could make many more mats of even more refined and beautiful style if she modified the weaving machine properly and got better rushes, and that for this purpose she would like to request a subsidy from His Highness.

"Concerning this matter," she added, "I have here something in which I have written down my ideas," and she took out of her kimono sleeve the parcel of five volumes. "I beseech you to give this material special consideration and look at it by yourself."

Ichi then lifted her face, tore off the silk patch disguise pasted on her cheek, and advanced on her knees, looking at the lord. A voice shouted, "Insolent woman!" Chikara Toda barred her path and two of the vassals in attendance stood up.

Ichi gazed straight into the lord's eyes and cried, "It's a matter of the greatest importance to your royal house. Please look at it with your own eyes. Please!"

The two vassals who had stood up arrested her. Toda grimaced unpleasantly, but stopped when Ichi was arrested. It was her good fortune that the major vassal in attendance, Chikara Toda, had not been involved in the political fight. If he had been a member of the Otaka clique, things would not have worked out so easily for her. At his shout of "Stop!" all the men, with the exception of the one grasping Ichi's shoulder, refrained from touching her.

"I'll look at it. Bring it here," the lord said quietly. He had a deep, very youthful voice.

One of his vassals took the parcel and handed it to him. He opened it, saying, "Let her go." Then he looked at the title of each volume and skimmed its contents with seeming lack of interest. After that he rewrapped the parcel and put it by his side.

"I permit you to answer my question directly. From whose family do you come?"

"I am the wife of an obscure man of no social position."

"Do you know the details of what is written here?" he asked in a very business-like tone, as if he did not care whether she knew or not. "Did someone tell you to petition me?"

"Being a woman, I know nothing about the details of this matter. I merely wanted, as his wife, to be my husband's successor and emulate his sincerity. He often said that he would sacrifice his own life for your royal house, the government, and the citizens and farmers of your clan. No one told me to do this; it was my own decision, made after I received permission to have the honor of an audience with you."

"I ask you once again. Whose wife are you?"

"He is of very low social position. Please forgive me . . ."

She broke off, and fell senseless to the ground. A voice said, "Look after her," and someone seemed to be supporting her. But she felt that she was falling down into jet black, angry waves and that her whole body was being turned around. She was drowning, she thought, and realized that at least she had to help Nobu, and she tried to push the child in her arms up to the surface of the water.

That was all she remembered. The power which had been sustaining her melted away, and she fainted.

18

SHE WAS told that as many seven days had elapsed before she regained consciousness. Old Josuke of Ogasa was the first of her visitors whom she remembered. His wife, Gen, had nursed Ichi for five days and two sleepless nights, but Ichi's recollection of Gen was confounded with that of her mother-in-law, who took turns watching her after that. She was told that she had persistently begged everyone to sell her combs and hair pieces and to give the money to Iso, but Ichi had no recollection of this at all. At this point people had begun to worry about Iso for the first time, and they tracked her down through Mozaemon in Morishima and brought her to Minojin House.

Kyunosuke had been a frequent visitor before she recovered consciousness, but the brother whose face remained most vivid in Ichi's memory was Tatsuya. He had sat at the head of her bed, his fat knees crossed, smiling with his usual easygoing expression, and told her many things.

"You know, I made a field on the roof this time, because those chaps called crops need sunshine and blowing wind. Then I'll be able to grow a big turnip. They say that turnip and catfish don't like metal. . . . They say we should wear straw sandals during floods. I was told we could get through the flood rather easily if we fix red clog thongs to them. I made some and brought them here, so you'd better put them on. I made some for Nobu—it's all right, as there's a flood."

Another time he had brought a big paper sack. "You see," he had said, "I caught all the mosquitoes in our house. So now it's all right to break down the walls."

When she was finally able to determine that the person now sitting at the head of her bed was Iso and that she was lying in a room at Minojin House, Tatsuya was the first person Ichi inquired about.

"So Tatsuya was saved after all. I'm so glad," she said.

"You know, Kyunosuke has been here," Iso said smiling, avoiding Ichi's question. "He's very sunburned, has got fat, and looks like a farmer, doesn't he?"

Ichi knit her brows and tried to remember. Kyunosuke . . . she thought she had seen him, but then maybe not . . .

Iso realized that she was disturbing Ichi by saying things she did not need to say, and tried to talk around the subject.

"Well, well, go back to sleep," she said as she changed the wet towel on Ichi's forehead. "Since you're still tired you shouldn't think about anything. . . . Just feel relieved and sleep. Everything's going to be all right. There's nothing for you to worry about."

Twelve or thirteen days after that, Ichi thought, Iso disappeared. Either a housemaid, or Josuke's wife, Gen, began to sit at her bed as Iso's replacement. Mankichi came to see her many times every day, and Teijiro also visited her once in a while. His face was always pale and dispirited, and he looked as if he wanted to complain to her about his worries but could not bring himself to talk about them. Instead of inquiring about Ichi's health, he merely sat for a while and left without a word.

Around that time she discovered that she was likely under house arrest, for officers from the deputy's office were in attendance in the next room and a doctor, also from the deputy's office, came daily to examine her.

During this time the repairs to the weaving shop were finished, and six new weaving machines were purchased with clan assistance. Four of the machines were for Ichi, and three girls, it was said, had been hired as her assistants.

"Could I possibly do such work while I'm under house arrest?" When Ichi spoke to Mankichi about her doubts, he shook his head, saying that actually she was by no means under house arrest. "When you're completely recovered and are able to sit at the machine, the daughters of the clan's samurai families are supposed to come here from Ogaki to take lessons from you."

Early one evening, an evening of cool autumn breezes shortly after Ichi had begun getting up for brief periods, Kyunosuke came to visit. The officers in the next room had now begun leaving in the afternoon, and weavers who used to be friendly with Ichi came to chat with her in the evening. Ume in particular was very much attached to her and said eagerly that she was going to be Ichi's first pupil no matter what anyone else said or did.

Kyunosuke's garb was a cross between farmer's and merchant's dress, and he was carrying a fan. He was sunburned, had grown stout, and looked just like Tatsuya when he smiled.

"Please stay as you are . . . please remain lying down," he said, and sat down at the head of the bed, looking cramped. "I heard you're getting much better. Your complexion has improved tremendously. I'm relieved."

"You've gained weight too."

"I'm surprised about that myself. I've been walking the chalk line between life and death, yet I look as if I've been eating the bread of idleness and fooling away my time. But of course, if I compare my hardships to yours, sister, I guess that's just about the case." He put his hands on his knees and bowed his head, gazing into Ichi's eyes. "It's hard to say it as it should be said, . . . but thank you very much, sister."

"I'm so happy to see you alive, Kyunosuke. I knew what a hard time you were having."

"Sister, . . . no, I shouldn't talk about this yet." He suddenly raised his head. "I want to explain all that has happened after everything has settled down and I can take my time. I intended to tell you after I found out how well you were, but I have to go to Edo again."

"You say 'again.' Then you were in Edo all the time after it happened?"

"No, I've been going back and forth. I even pretended to be a beggar—what a show! I intended to go to Ogasa, too, but the security watch was so strict I couldn't even get near the place. If there hadn't been this confusion about the flood, I wouldn't be here even now. Oh, about the flood . . ."

He was suddenly upset and coughing violently, waving his hand. "Oh, that's right, I have something to apologize to you for. You know, I often importuned you for pocket money, didn't I, sister? It has to do with that."

"What are you talking about now?" Ichi realized what Kyunosuke was going to say and why he had broken off. She smiled and went along with his game nonchalantly. "You're too smart to start begging from me again!"

"Oh, no, I'm not going to beg, I'm going to tell you the truth. I wasn't begging for pocket money to spend—I was saving it to give you a present, sister." He blushed in embarrassment, and put his hand to his neck. "Do you remember a fancy shop called 'Monhachi' in Kyomachi? They had for sale a red-lacquered toilet case with a gold decorative pattern. It was as large as this . . ." he gestured with his hands, "and the red-and-gold combination was inexpressibly beautiful; but the price was so high I simply couldn't buy it by saving only my pocket money. But I really wanted to make you a present of it. So, as a last resort, I started begging from you."

"I'm happy to hear that," Ichi smiled at him. "But if that's the case, I think I'll have to invest much more capital before I receive the toilet case!"

"No, you don't have to worry. I'm so sorry, but during all the commotion the case was sold. I had made a deposit on it, but since I hadn't made any payments in six months . . . surely someday . . ."

"Oh no, no, thank you." This time Ichi really laughed. "Your good intention alone is enough. I'll accept a present from you after you succeed in life."

After an hour Kyunosuke left. She had been waiting for the conversation to turn to her husband's case, but it did not. She had been afraid to ask about him, fearing that any inquiries might make her seem too much attached to her husband. But just before his departure Kyunosuke said, "I think the situation seems to be turning out favorably," and this was Ichi's most encouraging hope.

She had already given up hope for Tatsuya. Since she had seen him and heard his words so clearly and vividly during her illness, for a long time she had been sure of their reality. But because of her mother-in-law's attitude, or because she had heard nothing about Tatsuya from Josuke and his wife, she could not deny that it was an illusion, that he had met with disaster somewhere on the day of the flood, as she had feared.

What Ichi found unbearable was the thought that he had met that disaster when he went out to look for her. Might he have approached close to danger in his excessive worry over her and been driven to despair when he found out that it was too late? The most unbearable of all her fantasies was the thought of Tatsuya's face at that moment, with its lost look. He would have gazed around with his easy yet flustered expression and murmured, "I guess it's rather hopeless." Ichi could visualize him doing just that, and every time she thought of him she felt as if she were suffocating.

"I've learned that the appointment of the heir has been announced," Mankichi told her one day. "They say it's Einoshin, the second son of the Matsudaira family of Tatebayashi in Kozuke—Echi-Matsudaira, they're called—and that he'll soon come to pay his respects."

"To pay his respects, you say? That must mean Lord Toda is ill."

"I guess inspecting the flood district affected his health. They say he's been confined to bed for quite some time, and there's also a rumor that he's in critical condition."

This story gave Ichi something new to worry about. If the lord was sick in bed and in critical condition, what would become of the investigation into those five volumes of records? If the heir from Tatebayashi was the person recommended by her husband's allies, everything would be all right. But if he had been supported by the clique of Otaka, chief vassal of the clan, she had to judge that all was lost. Since either event would determine her destiny, Ichi's worry was by no means a petty one.

Soon after the news of the heir's appointment, more than ten officers from the deputy's office began guarding her. However, it looked more as if they were guarding all of Minojin House rather than overseeing Ichi. Later she found out that the investigation of the Otaka clique had begun at Ogaki castle, and it was said that Lord Toda had ordered a guard placed around Ichi.

The first two weeks of August came and went. Fall had begun.

19

ICHI, NOW completely recovered, started working on the weaving machines as soon as she had left her sickbed. She was stopped and told to start only after she had more fully recuperated, but she persisted because working on the machines distracted her from her worries. She began to weave the mats slowly, teaching the technique to Ume and the girls who had now been hired. The officers kept close watch over the people coming and going, and thus there was almost no communication with the outside world. Since she had not had an opportunity in a long time to see Josuke and his wife, she could not even find out how her mother-in-law was.

"Anyway, I've done the best I could," she consoled herself. "Good or bad, it's no use struggling any longer." She became completely absorbed in her work.

At the beginning of September a messenger came from Ogaki castle with an order to appear at the castle in the company of Teijiro. Thirty guardsmen and a carriage were provided for her. Ichi, seeing that half of them were armed with matchlocks, vacillated in her estimate of whether this was a good or a bad omen and was almost ashamed of the way she trembled while she was getting ready.

"I think I'll probably be able to come back soon," said Ichi, gazing into the face of each girl in the weaving shop as she said her farewells. "Even if I can't come back, if you make your design based on what I taught you, you should be able to make fine flower mats. Patience and the desire to make good things are the most important factors. Please don't get bored—help each other, work at it. . . . Ume, young as you are you must try to help the others, since you're the one most familiar with the work. I'm counting on you."

She felt almost as if she were expressing her last wishes, exaggerated as the idea was. They all came out to the gate to see her off. The vision of Ume, who had come out to the road and was constantly wiping the tears off her cheeks with her apron, remained in Ichi's memory for a long time.

As she was about to cross over from Karasue, she saw the stream of the Ibi River and its long dike in the far distance. A year ago she had walked with her mother-in-law and Tatsuya along this dike. She could recollect so vividly the confusion of that time, the feeling of being pursued, and her loneliness and uneasiness, as if it were only yesterday. When she closed her eyes she could see Tatsuya, who had been talking in such a casual manner about catfish. Ichi wiped away her tears and softly recited the Buddhist prayers for the dead for Tatsuya.

It took them four hours to travel seven miles. Shortly before four o'clock in the afternoon they reached the southeast gate of Ogaki, where three samurai took charge of them. Then Ichi and Teijiro were escorted to an antechamber in the Shinoda citadel around Ogaki castle. After they had tidied themselves and waited for a while, they were taken to the main castle.

The treatment accorded them after their arrival in the castle was not the type of treatment given to people who are to be punished. Ichi, who had been brought up in a samurai family, was aware of this, and the worry and doubt which had been nagging at her mind finally lessened. She heaved a sigh of relief and felt a cheerful expression come over her countenance.

Teijiro and Ichi sat down on a straw mat provided for them in the garden, with two officers in attendance on each side. The setting sun of late summer dyed the eaves of the palace red, and a red dragonfly rested its wings on the broad step with an air of enjoyment, warming its body in the waning daylight. The scene aroused a lonely, empty feeling of autumn at its peak.

At the sound of quick steps coming down the corridor, Ichi and Teijiro bowed their heads. Although they could not see, it seemed to be three people, judging by the sounds they made as they took their places. Soon one of them called Teijiro's and Ichi's names, and, after they had answered, another person quietly rustled a piece of paper.

"Ichi, resident of Shimada village, Yoro district

of our clan, dependent of Teijiro," the person read, "you have endured hardships and have behaved dutifully to your mother-in-law after separation from your husband due to an unforeseen event, despite ample reason to withdraw your presence . . ."

The voice described both her successful effort, after Minojin House had hired her, to produce a competent piece of work despite her lack of experience and also her creation of a beautiful flower mat the likes of which had never before been seen. As she listened, Ichi began to tremble in amazement. The voice had the powerful, quiet tone and characteristic clear intonation of her husband's. His voice seemed to have become somewhat husky and deeper than before, but she felt that her awareness of the change was indeed proof that it was her husband's voice. Her hands, as she lay prostrate, trembled violently.

"And during the flood in July you paid no heed to your beloved child in the emergency, but risked your own life to save your elderly mother-in-law. Although this was no more than your duty, still your noble intention is especially admirable. Therefore, His Highness bestows ten pieces of white gold and one kimono upon you. Signed, Shinzo Kugata, Chamberlain."

Ichi caught her breath and lifted up her face. It was indeed her husband who was sitting on the veranda and gazing at her as he rolled up the proclamation. As she looked at his firm shoulders under the linen formal kimono, his broad forehead with the clear hairline, and his lips which revealed the depth of his feeling,

Ichi's body shook with such violent passion that only with great difficulty did she restrain herself from flying to him.

Shinzo added calmly, "You may stay at your house in the castle town tonight." To Teijiro he expressed his praise for the master's special service—his good care of Ichi and his production of a flower mat unparalleled in any other country. He urged Teijiro to try to work at this project and develop it as a speciality of the clan, and promised him various rewards.

Ichi was listening attentively to each word with all her senses and nerves, as if absorbing everything he said. She could not understand the meaning of the words; all she wanted was to thoroughly grasp and absorb his voice itself, to melt into it body and soul.

The color of the sky was deepening into dusk by the time she returned to her beloved house in the castle town. She walked through the dear old gate, and as she approached the front door the servant Yagobei came out to meet her.

"Oh, are you back?" Ichi was about to say, when Iso came running out. "Mother!" Ichi stretched out her hands and ran to her.

"Welcome back! Welcome back!" Iso took her daughter-in-law's hands and smiled. "You've finally come back! Are you completely better? I think you look thinner."

"Oh, no. On the contrary, I've gained weight." She walked into the hallway, still holding her mother-in-law's hands. "When I try to tighten my obi it slides up like this. I've become like a young girl around here—I'm rather embarrassed. . . . Yagobei is back, isn't he?"

"Yes, and Wakichi and Heisuke, and Hana too—they're all back. I heard that Kyunosuke will be coming back at the end of the month."

When she walked into the living room and sat down, the servants assembled to greet her. Immediately after their withdrawal, Shinzo entered.

Upon hearing a servant announce him, Ichi stood up, almost instinctively. She felt surprised that her attitude had not changed in the slightest from what it had been before the events, and that her present actions were linked to those of the earlier time as naturally as if nothing had happened, as if the blank space of one year had not existed. As she received her husband's sword in the front room and followed him into the living room, Ichi was thinking, Everything's the same as before. Everything is going to settle down as before; the storm is over.

When Ichi had lit the lantern and brought him tea, Shinzo told her to sit down and looked into her eyes. She lifted up her eyes for the first time. Except for the voice of her mother-in-law, who was in the kitchen giving orders to Hana, it was perfectly still in the house.

Shinzo gazed at his wife's face warmly for a long time. Then he quietly bowed his head and said in a low voice that was almost a murmur, "I'm sorry to have given you so much trouble. What I want to thank you for, aside from looking after my family, is your direct petition to the lord for us. We were doing our best. The problem of the succession was moving in the direction we expected. But if that record had not come into Lord Toda's hands, I think we would have had more victims among our confederates, and the conflict would have gone on for a while longer. The delivery of that record at that particular time was of invaluable help to us. I extend to you my appreciation on behalf of those who died for this cause, those who were imprisoned, and the many people who worked for us, all but sacrificing their own lives and living in concealment. Ichi . . . thank you."

Putting her hands on her knees, and bowing her head, Ichi received his words humbly. Shinzo stopped talking, took out a tissue paper, and wiped his eyes softly.

"I shan't talk to you about other minor things, or about my mother," he said then, "but I'm sure you know what I'm thinking. But just one thing, about Nobu . . ."

Shinzo suddenly shifted forward and took his wife's hands. Ichi felt giddy, and a strange feeling overcame her. She began to weep violently and laid her face on her husband's knees. The fact that she had lost her own child had struck her for the first time. Up to this moment she had unconsciously been avoiding thoughts of her child and had been constantly turning her mind to other things. But now that she had met the man to whom she could speak of her sorrow, now that she could really share her grief, a wailing cry tore from her throat like a torrent breaking a dam.

"I wanted to see her—even if only once."

"I'm sure she wanted to see you. . . . It's a pity that she couldn't."

"You at least did what you could for her, but I . . ."

"My dear, my dear!"

"I couldn't even hold her in my arms."

Ichi wept on her husband's knees, pressing her cheeks against his hands. She did not think that she was behaving indecently or disgracefully; she felt she should cry as much as she could, as a kind of ceremony for the dead . . . for Nobu.

"Nobu, come back here. Come back here, between your father and mother. Here, this is your father's knee."

* * *

Epilogue

A FEW MINOR things should be added to complete the story: the punishment of chief vassal Kokuro Otaka, the resolution of the Okumura problem, Kyunosuke's return home, the succession of the adopted heir after Lord Toda's death, and the installation of a new government.

But all of these things can be left to the reader's imagination. Our purpose was merely to tell about Ichi.

ABOUT THE TRANSLATORS

MIHOKO INOUE received a multinational education, studying first in Japan, then in Europe and the United States, where she received her B.A. degree in philosophy. Her interests in philosophy and languages and her wide experience give her excellent qualifications for translating works like *The Flower Mat*. She presently lives in her native Tokyo.

EILEEN B. HENNESSY is a translator with ten books to her credit. Her interests in the field of philosophy, in art history, and in languages led her to study, work, and travel extensively in Eastern and Western Europe and the Middle East. A New Yorker, Miss Hennessy lives and works in the town of Setauket.